Carl Arnold Kortüm, Charles Timothy Brooks

Jobsiad

A grotesco-comico-heroic poem

Carl Arnold Kortüm, Charles Timothy Brooks

Jobsiad
A grotesco-comico-heroic poem

ISBN/EAN: 9783337213855

Printed in Europe, USA, Canada, Australia, Japan

Cover: Foto ©Andreas Hilbeck / pixelio.de

More available books at **www.hansebooks.com**

The Jobsiad

A

GROTESCO-COMICO-HEROIC POEM

FROM THE GERMAN

OF

Dr. Carl Arnold Kortum

BY

CHARLES T. BROOKS

TRANSLATOR OF "FAUST," "TITAN," ETC., ETC.

PHILADELPHIA:

FREDERICK LEYPOLDT.

LONDON:—TRÜBNER & CO.

1863.

TRANSLATOR'S PREFACE.

CARL ARNOLD KORTÜM, the author of this unique poem—which may almoſt be ſaid to form a genus by itſelf—was born at Mühlheim in 1745, and died as Phyſician, at Bochum, a ſmall town in Weſtphalia, in 1824, in the eightieth year of his age. If we knew the particulars of his life, we might perhaps find in him an anſwer to Solomon's queſtion in regard to laughter: "What doeth it?" namely, It prolongeth man's days.

The *Jobſiad* enjoys a great and general popularity in its native country,* and is, of courſe, a particular

---

* In Marggraff's *Houſe-treaſury of German humor* occurs the following:—

"The *Jobſiad* firſt appeared anonymouſly in 1784, and has now reached its Tenth Edition, [of ſeveral thouſand copies each] which may well be regarded as a proof of the power of this jolly book to ſtand the teſt of time. A book may attain to ſeveral editions in ſwift ſucceſſion, and then after all be ſuddenly forgotten or no more read; but when, after half a century, new editions of a book are ſtill called

favorite of ſtudents, ſeveral of whom the tranſlator has
heard recite paſſages from it—"pompouſly ſquaring
the circle deſcribed by the wrinkle round the mouth,"
as Jean Paul ſays of Schoppe—with exceeding rich-
neſs of comic effect.   Perhaps, indeed, to be perfectly

---

for and paſs out of print again,—this is certainly a proof of
its having a kernel of national and laſting vitality.   The
Jobſiad owes the popularity which it ſtill continues to find
as well to its draſtic drollery in the invention and management of characters and ſituations, and their ethico-hiſtorical
intereſt, as to the circumſtance, that pedantry, with its in-
numerable abſurdities, (which, indeed, forms the main object
of this comic poem) has not even to this day died out in
Germany, and will hardly ever die out, though it ſhould
from time to time aſſume different forms.   The treatment
betrays an original *vis comica* and a naive drollery ſuch as
are at this day ſeldom found; nay, the comic riſes ſome-
times even to humor, inſofar as we may regard it as one of
the peculiarities of humor, that the Poet toſſes about the
world, which he ſees at his feet, with ſovereign caprice, with
an ideal whimſicality, that never ſuffers itſelf to be degra-
ded, by the follies on which it exerciſes its perſiflage, to the
level of hypochondriacal moodineſs or a ſchoolmaſter-like
pedantry. . . . . .   The *Jobſiad* owes a great part
of its effect to the peculiar doggerel, ſince become typical,
managed by him with the moſt riotous extravagance of
whimſy, and yet at the ſame time with the ſure hand of a
maſter, which Kortüm, with happy hit, himſelf originally
created for his epic."

enjoyed and appreciated, ſuch a produ&ion ſhould be heard as read by ſome one who has the ſkill and ſpirit to give it the proper tone and *twang*, or, perhaps, it might advantageouſly be accompanied with a ſcale of muſical and *naſal* intonation.

By way of giving the reader all the help the caſe ſeems to admit, in the abſence of the deſiderata juſt referred to, the tranſlator will add a few remarks in reſpe& to rhyme and rhythm.

It will be obſerved, as one **of the commoneſt re-**quirements in making out the meaſure **and ſecuring** the comic effe&, that all ſorts of liberties **are taken,** for inſtance, with accent. **Thus, for the ſake of rhyme,** ſuch words as *Baron*, *Turkey*, *Father*, and many **others, have** the ſtreſs transferred to the laſt ſyllable; **and** ſo, too, *frequently*, *contrary*, **neceſſary**, will ſome-**times** have the emphaſis thrown on the laſt ſyllable but one.—Equal licence is allowed **in ſpelling.** *Swabia* is ſpelt *Swaby* to rhyme with **baby.** *Nature* is ſpelt *Natur* to rhyme with *Senater*. **The final *g* is repeat-**edly cut off from participles. Thus *ſpinning* becomes *ſpinnin'* for the ſake of making it rhyme with *women.* —But **the** reader's Yankee ſenſe will **do** juſtice **to all** theſe things as he goes along, and pra&ice will **beget** ſmoothneſs, the rough quality being gradually worn off by the fri&ion and heat of a rapid movement.

One word more in regard to the metre of this ram-
pant doggerel, and the tranflator, with the author, com-
mits his work to the "indulgent reader." The metre
is certainly fomewhat *particular metre.* The fhorteft
and moft fatisfactory key to be given for the fcanning
is to fay, boldly, that each line confifts of four feet,
each foot containing as many or few fyllables as the
cafe may require. We will give a fpecimen, trufting
that the reader will then feel compétent to career
with great rapidity, precifion and fatisfaction over the
roughneffes that moft ferioufly

<blockquote>"· Shake the rackt axle of Art's rattling car,"</blockquote>

and the occafional extended tracts of verfe, that might
otherwife prove to fome readers in this faft age a
dead man's journey.

Take, then, the following, which we divide, thus :—
(the odd fyllable over and above the four feet in the
firft couplet being a mere flourifh, or *kick-up* of the laft
foot—the hind foot, fo to fpeak, of the *quadruped*):—

"If ōne | of his pā | tients chānced | to recōv | er,
| It was trūm | petēd | the coūn | try ō | ver,
And they sāid | behōld ! | the fū | mous mān |
Has wroūght | a wōn | drous cūre | agūin. !

"But if he happened to lofe his patients,
Or they died in the midft of his operations,
'Twas then : He died for want of breath,
There's not an herb growing 's a cure for death."

The *Jobſiad* will already have had a certain introduction and commendation in this country by the four genial pictures of Hafenclever, now in Philadelphia, the firſt reprefenting Jobs as he comes home to his aftoniſhed family from the Univerſity, the ſecond as he appears before the Clerical Board of Examiners as a candidate for the miniſtry, the third, as a fchoolmaſter, and the fourth, as night-watchman. Thefe pictures were for a long time on exhibition at the Düfseldorf Gallery in New York, and the two chapters of this tranſlation containing Jobs's letter to his parents for money, when he was at college, and the elder Jobs's anſwer, were printed in full in the catalogue of the exhibition, having originally appeared, (the firſt and only portion of the *Jobſiad* ever printed till then in Engliſh) in the "Literary World," at that time under the taſteful, ſpirited and generous management of the brothers Duyckinck, whoſe kindneſs the tranſlator here gratefully remembers.

CONTENTS.

(xiii)

B

CHAPTER VI.

CHAPTER VII.

CHAPTER VIII.

CHAPTER IX.

CHAPTER X.

CHAPTER XI.

CHAPTER XII.

CHAPTER XIII.

CHAPTER XIV.

CHAPTER XV.

CHAPTER XVI.

CHAPTER XVII.

CHAPTER XVIII.

CHAPTER XIX.

CHAPTER XX.

CHAPTER XXI.

CHAPTER XXII.

CHAPTER XXIII.

CHAPTER XXIV.

CHAPTER XXV.

CHAPTER XXVI.

B*

CHAPTER I.

Preface, and the Author sets out to describe the story of Hieronimus Jobs, deceased, and he gives his little book the paternal benediction.

R ESPECTED READER! for thy edification,
And likewife for my own recreation,
    A fuperfine hiftory I plan,
    Of Hieronimus Jobs, a remarkable man.

2. Of whom I have many things to mention,
   Deferving your particular attention,
      And who, in all this life's queer mufs,
      Was a curious Hieronimus.

3. To tell all about him were out of the queftion,
   'Twould be too much for the reader's digeftion,
      And paper and fpace would be quite too fmall
      To recite his adventures each and all.

4. I have refpecting him many Data,
   But confine myfelf to the prominent Fata,
      And tell what he did from the day of his birth
      That was moft memorable on the earth.

5. Now, as I have received from St. Apollo
   The laudable gift of rhyme, it will follow
      That inftead of telling my tale in profe
      A very fine kind of verfe I chofe.

6. I may not always adopt that meafure
   In which a cultivated ear finds pleafure;
      The indulgent reader will confider meanwhile
      That this is what they call the *popular ftyle.*

7. From my anceftor, old Hans Sachs, I inherit
   As a fecond nature, the rhyming merit,
      Hence it is that I hold poefy fo dear,
      And relate all things in verfes here.

8. There's nobody but that rehearfes
   My coufin, the Wandfbeck meffenger's verfes,
      And yet, compared with my fabric, you'll find
      That his are very far behind.

9. I have at the fame time labored bufily,
   As the indulgent reader will fee very eafily,
      To have the book, as was right and good,
      Adorned with fine engravings in wood.

10. But as new engravings were fcarce and coftly,
    I have borrowed from other fources moftly,
       And yet it would puzzle any one to tell
       That they *were* borrowed, they fit fo well.

11. They're none of Chodowiecki's chefs-d'œuvre,
    I almoft flatter myfelf, however,
       They will do as well, or well enough,
       To help the book through a world fo rough.

12. And, then, if the pictures are not the neateft,
    The verfes, too, are not the completeft,
       And fo the two exactly agree
       And make out a perfect harmony.

13. And now little Book, I'll no longer delay thee;
    Go hence, to the fons of men difplay thee;
       There's many a book no better than thou,
       Is yearly fent to the Fair, I trow.

14. And yet allow me one moment to linger,
    While I place on thy head my authorial finger,
       And like a father benignantly,
       Pronounce, dear Book, a blefling on thee!

15. May heaven protect thee a good long feafon
    From critics, moths and lamp-paper treafon,
       And all other mifchiefs that await
       Printed books at the prefent date.

16. Thou wilt have, both in and out of Swaby,
    Thy native land, many readers, may be ;
        That paper, printing and labor of brain,
        May not, God help us ! have been in vain.

17. Go now and with my greetings hie thee
    To all and each who read and buy thee,
        And to every worfhipful Reviewer,
        My fpecial compliments, be fure.

18. Tell them,(but foftly, that they may not be offended,)
    How they have often reviewed and recommended,
        Many a book before now,
        That was much worfe written than thou.

NOTES.

Stanza 8.   The *Wandfbeck meffenger* means that fimple-hearted old German, Claudius, born in 1743, who fo called himself and took for the motto of his papers, " *Afmus, omnia fua fecum portans.*" (Afmus, carrying all his poffeffions with him.)

Stanza 10.   And yet the *learned* reader will detect in the wood cut that heads this chapter, the traditionary picture of St. Luke, attended by the Ox, and writing his gofpel.

Stanza 11.   Chodowiecki was a famous German artift in this line, born at Dantzic in 1723.

CHAPTER II.

*Of the parents of our hero and how he was born, and
of a memorable dream which his mother had.*

B EFORE I go further, it is my intention,
  Of our hero's two parents to make mention,
  And a word or two muſt be alſo ſet forth
  Concerning his true place of birth.

1*

2. It was, then, a little town in Swaby,
   Where the parents lived who had this baby,
   　And there his father, Hans Jobs by name,
   　Was a counsellor of considerable fame.

3. He was rich in cattle and that sort of blessing,
   Beside our hero many other children possessing,
   　Of the male sex and female no less,
   　And lived, on the whole, in peace and happiness.

4. He had in wine some little dealings,
   Was an upright man in his walk and feelings,
   　Just both at home and in council hall,
   　And a great economist withal.

5. A genuine Lutheran in his religious persuasion,
   In philosophy neither Wolfian nor Cartesian,
   　Because in fact neither Wolf nor Kant
   　Nor any philosophy could he understand.

6. To study, however, he had somewhat attended,
   And for a whole year the gymnasium frequented,
   　And consequently, so far, knew much more
   　Than any worshipful counsellor had done before.

7. When poor folks came, he loved to befriend them,
   And for a pledge would gladly lend them,
   　And never charged more than ten per cent,
   　And was somewhat phlegmatic in temperament.

8. He was rather short and squat in stature,
   Was endowed with a great appetite by nature,
   　The newspapers he loved to read,
   　And smoked many a pipe of narcotic weed.

✝

THE

𝕷𝖎𝖋𝖊, 𝕺𝖕𝖎𝖓𝖎𝖔𝖓𝖘, 𝕬𝖈𝖙𝖎𝖔𝖓𝖘, 𝖆𝖓𝖉 𝕱𝖆𝖙𝖊

OF

𝕳𝖎𝖊𝖗𝖔𝖓𝖎𝖒𝖚𝖘 𝕵𝖔𝖇𝖘,

THE

CANDIDATE,

A

MAN WHO WHILOM WON GREAT RENOWN,
AND DIED

AS

Night-Watch in Schildeburg Town.

Throughout, beginning, end, and middle,
Adorned with wood-cuts, neat as a fiddle,
A gay historia, pithy and terse,
Writ in new-fashion doggerel verse.

9. And often when the gall ran over,
   Severe attacks of gout he would fuffer,
      And yet he always found himfelf able
      To take his place at the council table.

10. The mother was of refpectable ftation,
    The moft eloquent woman in the Swabian nation,
       Tall and virtuous and upright,
       And meek as a lamb—*at firft fight.*

11. Only, alas! as too often the cafe is
    Not only here, but in other places,
       She now and then, when it came in her way,
       Would wear the breeches, as they fay.

12. Now this occafioned no fmall vexation
    At times, and led to altercation;
       Yet on the whole did our two loves
       Live like a pair of turtle doves.

13. They had now for feveral years in fucceffion
    Received of children a yearly addition,
       And yet at the time of our ftory, 'twas plain
       Mrs. Jobs was foon to come down again.

14. And now, when her nine months were ended,
    And the time of delivery impended;
       The above Mrs. Jobs immediately went
       To make preparation for the important event.

15. Before, however, I go on with my hiftory,
    I muft ftop to mention a singular myftery,
       A dream, in fact, that one night befel
       This Mrs. Jobs of whom I tell.

16. We learn by experience oft repeated,
    That dreams are not to be lightly treated;
        Of that, dear reader, I prefently
        A notable proof will furnifh thee.

17. One night, as Mrs. Jobs lay fleeping,
    This wonderful dream into her head came creeping,
        That, inftead of a little child, was born
        Of her a great and mighty horn.

18. This horn fo mightily crafhed and founded,
    That Mrs. Jobs woke up aftounded,
        And often, after fhe awoke,
        About that horn fhe thought and fpoke.

19. A lady, to whom fhe applied for explanation,
    Gave her at the time this confolation,
        That thus the interpretation ran:
        Her child would certainly be a great man.

20. And that his voice his mouth would nourifh,
    And in the pulpit would greatly flourifh,
        For that was clearly and finely fhown
        By the monftrous horn with its mighty tone.

21. But we will not here be anticipating
    The fequel for which the reader is waiting,
        And fo I now return to the text
        And proceed to tell what happened next.

22. The mother laid all things ftraight in her chamber,
    And on the thirtieth day of September,
        Juft at the right time fhe had the joy
        Of giving birth to a little boy.

23. Was ever a father's happinefs greaṭer?
   And heavens! how proudly felt the Senátor!
   And how did he leap, when, blooming there,
   He saw before him a son and heir!

NOTES.

Stanza 2. *Swaby*, poetic licence for Swabia, juſt as wa
have *Virginny* for Virginia, and for Arabia, *Araby* (the
Bleſt.)

Stanza 7. Some points in this description of old Jobs will
remind the reader of "Old Grimes."

CHAPTER III.

*How Mrs. Jobs, in child-bed, received a visit from her
female friends, and what Ma'am Gossip Schnepperle
prophecied of the child.*

A ND so Mrs. Jobs, as we've juft been telling,
With her dear little Jobfey was keeping her dwelling;
    Clofe by her fide all fwaddled he lay,
    And thought of nothing and flept away.

2. 'Twere impoffible to defcribe the jubilation
    That filled all the Jobfian habitation;
        Neighbors and kinfmen came and went,
        And thofe that couldn't themfelves go, fent.

3. The chamber rang with a conftant alarum,
    As when the bees in the May month fwarm,
        And all the day long it was buzz, buzz, buzz,
        Round the dear little Hieronimus.

4. Exactly three days had now expired,
    Since Mrs. Jobs to her bed retired,
        When a mighty fwarm of women made free
        To invite themfelves to afternoon tea.

5. And of all thefe madams, to my thinking,
   Who came to Mrs. Jobs's tea-drinking,
      Though there was none whofe gifts were fmall,
      Ma'am Schnepperle's gift excelled them all.

6. Little Jobfey's father was her coufin ;
   The company talked of the weather, and a dozen
      Other matters of the fame kind,
      And the converfation was quite unconfin'd.

7. Next after madam's health they inquired,
   And to know how the baby was they defired,
      Whether he feemed to like his pap,
      And was a quiet little chap?

8. Then they began, in rotation, to raife him
   High in the air and *beft* him and praife him,
      And none could find fit words to exprefs
      Their fenfe of his uncommon prettinefs.

9. " My honored coufin," began Ma'am Schnepperle,
   (She fpoke through her nofe, but rather dapperly,)
      A learned man the child will be,
      That by his face I can plainly fee.

10. " I have read a book and admired it greatly,
    Which I took from the council library lately,
       About the art of Phyfiognomy,
       And everything, the how and why.

11. " And there was a dreadful lot of faces,
    Pious rogues with terrible grimaces,
       Learn'd dunces, profiles ugly and fair,
       And heads of animals, too were there.

12. " If I rightly remember what I read there,
    I think (almoft in fo many words) it faid there,
       That there is genius in fuch a phiz,
       As this little wry one of Jobfey's is.

13. " Nor fhould I fear to pledge his mother
    That the child will take to books one day or other;
       And, if he only lives long enough, he
       Will be a parfon, undoubtedly.

14. " His mighty voice that he lifts like a trumpet
    Shows that he one day will mount the pulpit."
       (N. B.—Juft here little Jobfey cried out
       As if he knew what they were talking about.)

15. Ma'am faid much more before fhe had completed,
    That cannot in this place be repeated;
       However fhe ended at laft, and then
       All the women fell in with a loud Amen.

16. And now when the vifit was finally ended,
    Each one her hand to Mrs. Jobs extended,
    And thanked her for the honour fhe had done,
    Then all returned to whene they'd come.

17. **Poor Mrs.** Jobs's head-aches were fhocking,
    But fhe was edified by Ma'am Schnepperle's talking;
    Efpecially as the world faid, fhe
    Was acquainted with aftrology.

NOTES.

Stanza 3. *Swarm* in the fecond line muft be pronounced with the Irifh r : *swarrm.*

Stanza 8. To *heft*, was a vulgarifm in New England, in the tranflator's boyhood, meaning to teft the heavinefs (*heft*) of a thing by lifting it.

Stanza 10. The book would appear to have been Lavater.

Stanza 14. *Trumpet* and *pulpit* make a fine *affonanza.*

Stanza 16. **The** reader will please remember the rule for scanning given in the preface.

2

CHAPTER IV.

*How the child was baptized, and how he was named
Hieronimus.*

WHEN a few days more had alfo tranfpired,
'Twas baptifm plainly the infant defired,
　　For his cries were piteous to hear,
　　And caufed his mother pain fevere.

2. Vainly they plied both breaft and bottle,
Nor would fugar dollies ftop his throttle,
　　But he kept up one inceffant fhriek
　　'Till one could no longer hear himfelf fpeak.

3. Therefore in Senator Jobs's habitation,
Provifion was made for the baptifmal collation,
　　And difhes of all forts were made or fent
　　That might adorn the facrament.

4. Twifts and rings and other fuch matters,
Were baked for the fupper and piled on platters,
　　Nor was there in wine, tobacco and beer,
　　Certainly any deficiency here.

5. Friends and relations, aunts, uncles and coufins,
Nurfes, acquaintances, neighbors by dozens,
　　When the hour arrived, came pouring in,
　　All fmiling and dreffed as neat as a pin.

6. That fexton and **parfon, with formulary,**
    Were alfo there, you need not query,
      And the whole fenatorial body, **too,**
      Had arrived at the houfe in feafon **due.**

7. Many other guefts alfo, by **invitation,**
    Came to this great and high celebration,
      And to Jobs's credit confeffed it **muft be,**
      That all paffed off with **propriety.**

8. However there rofe a difputation
    About the infant's appellation ;
      Whether Heinz it fhould **be, or Peter or Hans,**
      Or Joft or **Jacob or Hermann or Franz.**

9. But none of thefe names, though full of attraction
    Seemed to give univerfal **fatisfaction,**
      And matters might almoft have **paffed**
      From words to fomething **worfe at laft,**

10. Had not the parfon, with wife **difcerning,**
    Given this advice, like a man **of learning,**
      To examine **the calendar, and fee,**
      Affixed to the birthday what **name might be.**

11. The calendar, without further **queftion,**
    Was ftraightway **opened by the fexton,**
      And there they **found without any fufs,**
      The name of St. Hieronimus.

12. Such a wife counfel to all the connection,
    To parents and godfathers gave great fatisfaction,
      And **fo the vote** was unanimous,
      That the child fhould be called Hieronimus.

13. And now when this weighty point was decided,
    The parſon, in manner and form provided,
       Pronounced and performed the Actus, and thus
       The child was baptized Hieronimus.

14. **A**ll things thereafter went calm and coſy,
    Parſon and ſexton waxed right roſy,
       And **they** did nothing elſe for almoſt half
       The night but eat, drink, ſmoke and laugh.

CHAPTER V.

How the little child Hieronimus occupied himself.

WHILE yet in his fwaddling clothes, Hieronimuffy
  Paffed his time in a manner fufficiently fuffy,
    Slept, ate, fucked or drank, one after another,
    Or liftened the lullaby fung by his mother.

2. His fleeping and eating, and fucking and drinking,
    Were much like other children's, to my thinking;
      Much time in rocking him alfo was fpent,
      And yet for all that he was never content;

3. But often would fcream whole days together,
    And raife in the cradle a bitter pother,
      As if fome terrible grief had affailed him,
      Though there was nothing on earth that ailed him.

4. Some wife people have undertaken,
    With an air that implied they could not be miftaken,
      To affert that there muft in thefe cafes be
      (God save the mark!) fome forcery.

5. And fo the nurfe and eke the phyfician
    Are called to pronounce on the child's condition,
      And many a dofe of rhubarb and rum
      Is given, and fometimes laudanum.

2*

6. He thus became almoſt a burden to his mother,
   But he throve in this way as well as in any other,
   And every day, as it came along,
   Found him more fat and stout and ſtrong.

7. Father and mother took therefore great pleaſure
 . In their darling child—their precious treaſure,
   And many was the hearty buſs
   They gave little Hieronimus.

8. I have no further information
   Of the firſt few years of Jobs's earthly probation;
   And therefore it is beſt, I ſuppoſe,
   To bring this chapter here to a cloſe.

NOTE.

Stanza 5.   "What are you doing, mad mother! miſerable nurſe! when you pour this vile compound into the unſtained ſnow of an infant's boſom! Know you not that paregoric is opium and rum?   A compoſition that Samſon could not have ſwallowed much of, unſcathed." *Sermon on Intemperance.*

CHAPTER VI.

Actions and opinions of Hieronimus in his boyish years,
and how he went to school.

OF the other early years of our hero,
I likewife can give no information that is thorough,
 Inasmuch as the courfe his life has run,
 Has been hitherto a very narrow one.

2. Confequently an account of his actions,
 Would poffefs no remarkable attractions;
  Suffice it to fay, that while yet a boy,
  Eating and drinking were his chief employ.

3. He had however his gifts as well as others,
 Preferred as playmates the girls to their brothers,
  Would often quarrel and teafe in play,
  And was noted for many a mifchievous way.

4. Lying and fwearing he early took to,
 And learned them well without any book too,
  Whereby the neighbours' children round
  Much edification in his company found.

5. He had a fweet tooth, loved candy to diftraction,
 Likewife in nuts and raisins took great fatisfaction,
  And all the money he got and fpent,
  For fomething dainty and liquorifh went.

6. With brothers and fisters he always was quarrelling,
    But his father never would give him a feruling,
        And as to his mother, poor, dear, good soul
        She never noticed fuch things at all.

7. All children of his age he could mafter,
    There was none of them could leap or run fafter,
        Not one of them was fo ftrong as he,
        And whoever provoked him had better let him be.

8. And being a boy of great endowments,
    He was charged with many houfehold employments,
        To foddering the cattle would fometimes fee,
        And fuperintend the economy.

9. Sometimes he rode the horfes to water,

Or a jug of beer from the tavern brought, or
    A fresh laid egg from the hennery,
    Or a goose's or duck's, as the cafe might be.

10. On the whole, was a fair, good-for-nothing fellow,
     Had a pair of lungs that could terribly bellow,
       And would act on a bench the preacher's part;
       All this went right to his parents' heart.

11. For they watched with a fecret gratification
     Hieronimus's talent in its manifeftation,
       And often in their heads it would run:
       " There is the parfon, fure as a gun."

12. Efpecially the mother, who remembered
     The Schnepperle's words, when she was chambered,
       And alfo the dream fhe formerly had,
       Could hardly contain herfelf, fhe was fo glad.

13. For all feemed to hang together fo neatly,
     And exprefs the matter fo completely;
       And when fhe weighed all this, fhe could fee
       The future parfon as plain as could be.

14. Accordingly to fchool they fent him,
     To fit him for the ftation they meant him,
       Which pleafed Hieronimus little enough,
       For he liked his play much better than fuch ftuff.

15. He hated his leffons and never learned them,
     He threw his books on the floor or burned them,
       And the a, b, abs and the o, b, obs
       They gave a head-ache to mafter Jobs.

16. 'Tis true, the preceptor did earneftly endeavour
     To recommend learning to his favour,
       And he and the rod in company,
       Worked away at his genius faithfully.

17. This man had remarkable qualifications
    For giving felf-willed boys educations,
        And oftentimes on fhoulder and back
        His cane came down with a mighty thwack.

18. Extraordinary efforts in this cafe were needed,
    But at length the Herculean labor fucceeded,
        And Hieronimus his letters told,
        By the time he was about ten years old.

19. How old he may have been exactly,
    When he learned to read the German correctly,
        I am not at prefent prepared to ftate
        In a manner very accurate.

20. And when more years he began to reckon,
    From the German fchool the boy was taken,
        And to the Latin fchool was fent
        To learn his Latin ; but how it went

21. With Hieronimus in his Latin,
    And how they fucceeded in getting *that* in,
        All this I promife faithfully,
        The reader fhall in the next chapter fee.

CHAPTER VII.

*How the boy Hieronimus went to the Latin fchool, and
how he did not learn much there.*

H IERONIMUS, purfuing the parental intention,
Began now at Menfa his Firft Declenfion,
And every important article taught
In the Latin grammar he likewife got.

2. Many vocables he alfo committed,
   But the poor Hieronimus was much to be pitied,
   For that curséd loufy Latin, he faid,
   Would nowife get into his head.

3. In Conjugations and Syntaxis,
   And generally in the Latin Praxis,
   It feemed as if the old Harry was loofe,
   And his body fuffered no little abufe.

4. For the Rector being a Hypochondriacus
   Showed no partiality to Hieronimus,
   But cudgelled him often as if he were mad,
   And many a fkinfull he gave the poor lad.

5. By a fyftem of teaching fo painfully hurried,
   The youth almoft to death was worried,
   And often wifhed (in terms uncivil)
   His grim old Rector would go to the d——l.

6. 'Tis true, full many a trick he played him,
   And richly for all the cudgellings paid him,
   In fact the man had a deal of fufs
   With the rogue of a Hieronimus.

7. For he cut up incognito all forts of capers
   With the old gentleman's perukes and papers,
   And fent full many a poifoned dart
   Right into the worthy man's heart.

8. He gave his fchoolmates, too, much trouble,
   And brought them into many a hobble,
   For he hated them with hatred profound,
   And often knocked them flat on the ground.

9. No book of theirs, nor any garment
   Was fafe from the tricks of this torment,
   And many of his tricks were of that kind,
   That leave a very bad odour behind.

10. **Sometimes he** would act the eavesdropper,
    And catching a fchoolmate at anything improper,
    Straightway he to the Rector reported the boy,
    And witneffed the flogging with heartfelt joy.

11. Lazy in brain and fore in body,
    At length he went home quite fick of ftudy,
    And there for the moft part his time paffed by
    In unprofitable inactivity.

12. Of his Greek I have nothing to fay at prefent,
    He found it exceedingly unpleafant,
    And the barbarous Tupto, Tupteis,
    Would turn Hieronimus' heart **to ice.**

13. Far be it from me, thought he, to dabble
    In fuch a jaw-cracking, Irifh gabble,
    And as regards the Hebrew fpeech,
    He called it poifon and **kept out of its reach.**

14. He made therefore no **progrefs** worth repeating,
    Save in lying and fwearing and drinking and eating,
    And in the invention of an original cuss,
    Nobody could match Hieronimus.

NOTE.

Stanza **14**. *Cuss* is Yankee for *curse*. (*Note for foreign readers.*)

CHAPTER VIII.

*How Hieronimus's parents, with the Rector and other
friends, took counfel what they fhould make out of
the boy.*

Now when the boy in this ftate of diftraction,
Had paffed fome eighteen years and a fraction,
And in fact was already half a head higher
Than old Hans Jobs his fire,

2. His parents began to be puzzled with cogitation
About his future occupation,
For it was high time fomething fhould be done
With this moft extraordinary fon.

3. Firft of all they put the Rector the queftion,
Whether he could not make any fuggeftion
As to his future deftiny,
And what he was beft fitted to be.

4. Now this man would not diffemble in the matter,
Nor with idle hopes the parents flatter,
So he came out roundly and told the truth:
" You can't make anything good of the youth.

5. "Study is clearly not his vocation ;
   It were wifer to try fome occupation ;
      A Counfellor might of fuch a one be made ;
      If not, it were well to put him to a trade.

6. "I have many a time in recitation
   Difcovered with great commiferation,
      That there's nothing in him that poffibly could
      Do a refpected public the leaft mite of good."

7. This fpeech, as may well be apprehended,
   The Jobfian couple grievoufly offended ;
      They heaped upon it all manner of abufe
      And called the Rector a ftupid goofe.

8. In a council of friends the queftion was ftated,
   And pro et contra rationally **debated ;**
      Old Jobs looked as grave, and fo did all,
      As if that houfe were the council hall.

9. After they had been two-and-a-half hours in feffion
   They compromifed matters by this propofition :
      That the fubject be poftponed to a new term
      For *nearer examination ; meanwhile we adjourn.*

CHAPTER IX.

How the gipſy Urgalindina was alſo conſulted about Hieronimus, who underſtood the chiromantic art.

A ND now all the friends who the meeting attended,
At Counſellor Jobs's, homeward had wended,
    When, as good luck would have it, one day,
    There came an old gipſy along that way.

2. From a very old family ſhe was deſcended,
Urgalindina was her name, ſhe pretended,
    And Egypt, ſhe ſaid, was the country from which
    She came, and her mother was burned as a witch.

3. Men's actions and fortunes this woman predicted,
When ſhe the lines on their hands had inſpected,
    And future things as clearly could trace
    As if they already had taken place.

4. She had greatly delighted many a maiden
By propheſying her approaching weddin',
    And indicated the bridegroom's name
    As if ſhe had long been acquainted with the ſame.

5. To many an heir beginning to be diſcontented,
The ſpeedy death of a rich uncle ſhe hinted,
    And oh, how glad would ſuch a one be,
    When his uncle died unexpectedly!

6. To many almoſt deſpairing ſpouſes,
   Whoſe wives, alas! were the plagues of their houſes,
   She came with welcome words of **cheer**
   And whiſpered a ſpeedy deliverance near.

7. **To many a dunce** diſagreeably ſmelling
   Of muſk and pomatum, ſhe was often ſeen telling
   How, in ſpite of all his awkwardneſs,
   He would find ſome fair one his heart to **bleſs.**

8. The words ſhe choſe were always ſo fitting
   That ſhe hardly ever failed of hitting;
   Yet a cunning ambiguity
   Helped her out of many a perplexity.

9. **She had for each** ſome ſpecial good ſtory:
   To ſoldiers ſhe propheſied powder and glory,
   To deſtitute epicures heaps of gold,
   The kingdom of heaven to matrons old.

10. With other arts ſhe was alſo acquainted,
    But not all her ſingular merits prevented
    Her falling occaſionally into ſin,
    For ſhe ſtole, incidentally, now and then.

11. **In** short her reputation rivaled in ſplendor,
    The fame of the celebrated witch of Endor,
    At leaſt in lying and chiromancy
    No gipſy woman was keener than ſhe.

12. Now when Mrs. Jobs heard of her coming,
    She immediately went to find the woman,
    And at her door, juſt out of her reach,
    Addreſſed to her the following ſpeech:

13. "My dear Mrs. Urgalindina, right glad am
    I to fee you on the prefent occafion, Madam,
        I've a fon I beg that you would fee,
        And pronounce on his future deftiny.

14. "I truft you will yield to our perfuafion,
    And without any equivocation or evafion
        Very candidly ftate to us,
        What is to be done with Hieronimus."

15. "Madam!" fhe anfwered, "I will do as directed,
    So foon as I his hands have infpected;
        I will then, as an honeft woman, declare
        His future fortune, to a hair."

16. They immediately fent for Hieronimus,
    And Ma'am Urgalindina in a fomewhat ominous
        Tone, requefted his right hand to fee
        Which fomewhat fmutty happened to be.

17. The gipfy woman, with fearching vifion,
    Examined all points with great precifion,
        Meafured the lines and the furfaces too,
        As chiromantifts are wont to do.

18. For a moment or two fhe nothing uttered,
    At laft like a Delphian Sibyl fhe muttered
        Something between her teeth a while,
        And prophefied in the following ftyle:

19. "I've founded, my dear Hieronimus, I've founded,
    By the art in which I am perfectly grounded,
        Thy whole future deftiny, my fon!
        By that throat of thine and its mighty tone—

20. " Shall many a brazen villain be fhaken,
   Many a flumbering finner fhalt thou awaken,
     So that the city far and wide,
     Shall by thy gifts be edified.

21. " Both good and evil fhall feel thy protection,
   Thou fhalt guard from body's and foul's deftruction
     Both young and old, and great and fmall,
     A faithful and vigilant keeper to all.

22. " Thy wife teachings this city's population
   Shall one day hear with edification,
     And when thy mouth is opened to cry
     Aloud, no one fhall make reply.

23. " I may not for the prefent, venture
   Any farther than this on thy future to enter,
     But what I have faid muft now fuffice,
     Go then, my fon, now go and be wife."

24. Here Urgalindina her prophecy ended,
   Both father and mother, who had clofely attended,
     Were entirely fatisfied and filled with joy,
     To hear fuch prediction concerning their boy.

25. For in their minds already our hero
   Was clearly a parfon in futuro,
     With this the prophecy feemed to agree,
     How could it be clearer poffibly?

26. Off did Urgalindina hobble,
   When fhe had got a fumptuous fee for her trouble :
     They fay fhe had fcarcely got out of fight,
     When fhe laughed at parents and fon outright.

27. And now, to cover the Rector with confufion,
    Both Mr. and Mrs. Jobs came to the conclufion,
        That the beloved Hieronimus
        Should ftraightway become a Theologus.

28. In chapter Tenth, we fhall therefore accompany
    Hieronimus to the Academy;
        But firft we muft ftop awhile to tell
        What took place at the laft farewell.

NOTE.

Stanza 2.   The reader must be careful not to pronounce *witch* and *which* as if they were the same word, as school-boys sometimes do.

CHAPTER X.

How Hieronimus took leave of his parents and brothers and ſiſters, and started for the univerſity.

WHEN Hieronimus's departure was decided,
Straightway he was ſuperfluouſly provided
  With clothes, books, money and everything
  That is neceſſary to ſtudying.

2. The family found ſome conſolation
   In the labour and care of the preparation,
     But when the parting hour drew near
     On both ſides was many a bitter **tear**.

3. The grave old Senator Jobs's bawling,
   Was juſt a regular caterwauling,
     And ſobbing he gave a farewell kiſs
     To his dear ſon Hieronimus.

4. And he added alſo a fatherly bleſſing,
   This counſel to the youth addreſſing;
     "Farewell and attend to **thy** ſtudies, my ſon,
     That we may have joy, when all is done!

5. "If anything ſhould ever ail thee
   (There may be times when money will fail thee,)
       Always write without fear to me,
       Whatever is wanting I'll ſend to thee!"

6. Hieronimus was, as may well be ſuſpected,
   By his father's words extremely affected,
       And promiſed always to let him know
       Whenever his purſe ſhould be getting low.

7. Still worſe was it with the poor mother
   Who did not undertake her grief to ſmother;
       Pierced through by ſorrow's bitter dart,
       She preſſed her dear ſon long to her heart.

8. At length ſhe ſtepped aſide a ſecond,
   And to Hieronimus beckoned,
       And ſlipped into the hand of her ſonny
       A little bag containing ſome money.

9. This very pious motherly bleſſing
   Was to Hieronimus deeply diſtreſſing,
       And not without many a heavy ſob,
       He thruſt the little bag in his fob.

10. Next came his brothers and ſiſters in rotation,
    Whom he, amidſt piteous lamentation,
        Each by the hand ſucceſſively ſhook,
        And now his departure Hieronimus took.

11. The weeping and wailing of the parents laſted
    For ſeveral days; the old man faſted
        To ſuch an extent as utterly to refuſe
        Wine, beer, tobacco and the daily news.

12. The greateſt of all was the mother's trouble,
　　She was almoſt inconſoláble,
　　　But with the brothers and ſiſters, I hear,
　　　There was very much leſs danger to fear.

N. B.—The wood-cut that heads the next Chapter, admi-
rably fulfils the Author's promiſe in Chapter I, 10. The
double knave of cards expreſſes in emblem Hogier's gambling
and double-dealing. One of them being knave of *hearts*
alludes to the *affectionate* manner by which Hieronimus was
taken in, while the hanging of the head (Kopfhängerei)
betrays the hypocrite ; the other being the knave of diamonds,
intimates how he took all the profits as well as honors.
(Stanza 29.)

　　The Chriſtian, or rather Pagan name *Hector* in the firſt
card denotes the gay and brazen rogue, while that of *Hogier*
in the ſecond ſeems to refer to the *hoax*, the humbug, he
played off on Hieronimus.

CHAPTER XI.

*How Hieronimus came on horfeback to the poft-ftation,
and how he found at the inn a diftinguifhed gentleman, named Herr Von Hogier, who gave him whole-
fome leffons, and was a knave.*

AND now Hieronimus has finally departed;
The old houfe fervant who was very kind-hearted,
Rode to the next village by his fide,
Where he was to get into the poftwagon to ride.

2. Altho' now the departure had affected him fadly,
  Neverthelefs he looked forward **gladly**
    To the beloved univerfity,
    Where time paffes off fo pleafantly.

3. Scarcely had he began to find him-
  felf out on the highway and Schildburg **behind him,**
    When he parents and brothers and fifters forgot,
    And was highly delighted at the thought,

4. **That now henceforth, as a free ftudent,**
  He need be no longer fo prim and prudent,
    And as to the grim old Rector and his rod,
    He was well rid of them, thank **God!**

5. It filled him with fpecial exultation,
  He was richer than a king in his own eftimation,
    When the money into his mind did come
    Which he had taken with him from home.

6. He thought and he *felt* with the greateft pleafure,
  Of the little bag, the precious treafure,
    From his highly afflicted mother received
    When fhe at parting fo bitterly grieved.

7. And now, as all other paftime was wanting,
  He drew out the bag and fell to counting
    The money, and found to his happinefs
    That the little bag contained no lefs

8. Than thirty different pieces of money,
  All of filver, thick, heavy and fhiny,
    Gilders and dollars manifold,
    Moftly of coinage rare and old.

9. His mother had faved them one after another,
   And for future emergencies laid them together,
   For not unjuftly fhe had the name
   Of being an economical dame.

10. Then too the fervant who attended him
    By way of paftime occafionally handed him
    Some of the victualia
    His parents had provided **to eat on the way.**

11. **Now** when in this kind of occupation,
    Hieronimus had ridden fome hours in fucceffion,
    Faint and weary he at length got down
    At the tavern of the aforefaid town.

12. Here indeed he found the poftwagon
    In which to the univerfity he was to jog on;
    But it fo happened that the cart
    Was not at the moment ready to ftart.

13. Hieronimus firft of all directed,
    That his nag to the ftable fhould be conducted;
    The fervant put fome oats in the rack,
    And took the portmanteau off his back.

14. At the fame time he began to be thinking,
    Of refrefhing himfelf by eating and drinking,
    And foon to the table he found his way,
    And there grew ftrong and frefh and gay.

15. Now there was in the tavern a fellow lodger,
    With a great peruke, and a rich-looking codger,
    The man from diftant countries came,
    Herr Baron von Hogier was his name.

16. The ftranger fhowed our hero much honour,
     And inquired who he was in a friendly manner;
        Hieronimus anfwered without demur,
        " I am a ftudent, refpected fir,

17. " At your honour's fervice, and right glad am I
     That I am going to the academy,
        There to ftudy diligently
        The fcience of theology."

18. " Ah! well, I wifh you all the joy I can, fir!"
     The gentleman in the great peruke made anfwer,
        " But, I advife you, take great care
        That you do not get into trouble there.

19. " I in my time have had fome knowledge
     Of the way they carry on at college;
        · Many a young frefhman throws away
        His time and money on curféd play.

20. "And many, inftead of ftudying with application,
     Run into all manner of diffipation,
        And wafte their valuable time
        In many a folly, not to fay crime.

21. " My own experience can anfwer
     For this fad truth, indeed it can, fir:
        I beg you therefore to attend
        To what I fay, on the word of a friend."

22. " Dear fir," Hieronimus refponded,
     " I thank you for advice fo candid,
        And the timely wifdom you have taught
        Shall never in all my life be forgot.

23. "At the fame time I will not difguife the truth, fir,
   Playing has great attractions for this youth, fir,
     But I have the honor to affure you that I,
     Whenever I do play, never play high."

24. "In moderate playing I fee no danger,"
   Politely anfwered the diftinguifhed ftranger,
     "One lofes nothing, except ennui,
     And paffes the time quite pleafantly.

25. "We, for example, here together,
   For the fake of amufing one another,
     Might play a little game," faid he,
     "With innocence and propriety."

26. Hieronimus, without the leaft fufpicion,
   Accepted the gentleman's propofition,
     And was very willing to take a game
     Or two, until the poftwagon came.

27. The thing was done as foon as decided,
   The hoft a new pack of cards provided
     And placed before his guefts, and ftraightway
     The two fat down and began to play.

28. They fet their ftakes quite low in the beginning,
   But Hieronimus, led on by his love of winning,
     To mark up higher and higher begun,
     Becaufe at firft he regularly won.

29. But all on a fudden fortune deferted
   Our hero, with whom fhe had previoufly flirted,
     And the gentleman in the great peruke
     Both all the honors and profits took.

30. And thus Hieronimus had very foon parted
    With all the loofe money he took when he ftarted,
    And now as his loffes came thick and faft,
    He drew out the little bag **at laft.**

31. And now Hieronimus began to grow frightened,
    For at every throw the bag was lightened,
    And it became very evident that luck
    Would fmile on the gentieman in the great peruke.

32. In lefs than three-quarters of an hour the bleffing
    Of his poor dear mother was entirely miffing,
    For the gentleman in the great peruke
    Had robbed him of all by hook and crook.

33. For the good Hieronimus had not detected,
    In fact he never for a moment fufpected,
    That he was cheated by him of the great peruke,
    For Herr von Hogier had an honeft look.

34. At laft he really began to
    Think of unbuckling his portmanteau,
    To ftake the little therein **contained,**
    Which would his refources have entirely drained,

35. But at that moment fo highly ominous,
    The gentleman in the peruke and Hieronimus,
    Both heard on a fudden the poftillion blow,
    As a fignal for Hieronimus to go.

36. He felt a little reluctance at parting,
    Then fuddenly and impetuoufly ftarting,
    He jumped up into the poft-wagon and took
    Leave of the gentleman in the great peruke.

CHAPTER XII.

How Hieronimus took the Poſt-wagon, and how he found
therein a fair one with whom he fell in love, and who
ſtole his watch.

I WILL now proceed with a narration
Of what befel Hieronimus on leaving the ſtation,
    For he is not rid of his troubles yet,
    But further obstacles are to be met.

2. The great peruke would ſtill come gliding
  Into his thoughts as he went on riding,
    And he now for the firſt time began to ſee
    That the fellow no better than a knave could be.

3. His conſcience kept up a terrible racket
  About the loſs of the maternal packet,
    He ſighed and groaned and wiſhed bad luck
    To the gentleman in the great peruke.

4. He murmured ſo that people could hear him;
  But a beautiful damſel ſitting near him,
    On whom his eyes till now ſcarce fell,
    Rouſed him from the melancholy ſpell.

5. She feemed about twenty years—not older,
   Black eyes and hair and a very white fhoulder,
      Rofy-red in mouth and cheek
      And, the truth in a fingle word to fpeak,

6. Her being was nothing but grace, appealing
   Irrefiftibly to the tendereft feeling.
      This fairy inquired, half in jeft,
      What forrow difturbed Hieronimus' breaft.

7. Wherewith fhe pleafantly fmiled upon him,
   Which pleafant fmile of her's quite won him.
      So that, as clofe by her fide he fot,
      The lofs of his packet he quite forgot.

8. A glow of rapture kindled his fancies,
   For in her whole perfon and tender glances,
      A youth like him could not fail to find
      Something quite dangerous to his peace of mind.

9. After lefs than half an hour's duration
   He had made, in beft ftyle, a declaration
      As fervent as ever a hero of romance
      Can make to his love by his author's hands.

10. She feemed to hear him with fome predilection,
    At all events fhe made no objection,
       Hieronimus therefore edged up more near
       And began to whifper in her ear.

11. I know not what further paffed on the occafion
    Improper to mention in this narration,
       Suffice it, with both, the time paffed by
       In fweet, confidential familiarity.

12. When at laft they came to the poft-ftation
    She bade adieu with friendly proteftation,
        But in what direction fhe went from here
        Shall by and by be made to appear.

13. When, after feveral hours had tranfpired
    Since the fair one from the carriage retired,
        Hieronimus for his watch looked round,
        That too had retired and was not to be found.

14. This fecond trick of fatal termination
    Was to Hieronimus a great aggravation,
        For he came to the conclufion that she who left
        So fuddenly muft have committed the theft.

15. Meanwhile nothing was left the good ftudent
    But to exercife patience and be more prudent,
        In fhort he determined, come what might,
        To practife in future more forefight.

16. He therefore formed a firm determination,
    So foon as he fhould come to the place of education,
        A letter to his parents to fend,
        For a new watch and fome money to fpend.

17. At laft without further moleftation
    He arrived at the place of his deftination,
        Behold therefore our Hieronimus
        Henceforward an Academicus.

NOTE.

Stanza 3.   *Luck* muft be pronounced in a certain provin-
cial Englifh ftyle, to rhyme with *peruke*.

CHAPTER XIII.

How Hieronimus at the Univerſity did diligently ſtudy Theology.

HIERONIMUS on his arrival, without heſitation,
Received, ſtante pede, his matriculation,
  And ſo became immediately
  A ſtudioſus of theology.

2. At univerſities, from all points of the compaſs,
  Some to get knowledge and ſome to raiſe a rumpus,
    Great numbers of ſtudents together are flung,
    Large and little and old and young.

3. And ſo at this one from every nation
  Were many in ſearch of an education,
    And many new ones came every year
    To proſecute various ſtudies here.

4. *Exempli gratiâ*, law and theology,
  Philoſophy, medicine and coſmology,
    And whatſoever other fine arts
    Are needed to help them act well their parts.

5. But moſt of them, inſtead of pondering
  Their ſtudies, ſet themſelves to ſquandering
    Their money, fared ſumptuouſly every day
    And threw their precious time away.

6 Hieronimus who liked ftudy no better than others,
Soon joined himfelf to the merry brothers,
And very fhortly made it appear
As if he had long been familiar here.

7. For he daily lived in *Floribus*
As well as the beft academicus,
And many a precious night he fpent
In carroufing and boufing to his heart's content.

8. Wine, beer and tobacco were his infpiration,
And they gave his voice a fine inflation,
When he with loud and mighty clang
The *gaudeamus igitur* fang.

9. His fellows all who gathered round him
The model of a faithful ftudent found him,
He lived as a *burfch* of high renown
And great was his fame through all the town.

10. As to thofe three detefted creatures,
Philiftines and Beadles and night-rogue-catchers,
Hieronimus as a hero true
Had often cudgelled them black and blue.

11. Many a *Pereat* he againft them had vented,
And with ludicrous tricks their peace tormented,
And in thefe and various other ways
As a *renownift* acquired great praife.

12. The fummer he fpent in racing and riding,
And in winter was continually fleighing and fliding,
In fhort Hieronimus felt himfelf free
To indulge in all manner of luxury.

13. Often he went on a pleasure pillage
    To one or another neighboring village,
        And mostly where he was likely to find
        Some fair one sociably inclined.

14. To breaking **windows** nightly he was addicted,
    Many tricks on young *foxes* inflicted,
        Dice and cards and billiards played,
        And not much progress in learning made.

15. In rows and riots he found great enjoyment,
    Sleeping in taverns was his daily employment,
        But twice in every month or so,
        To college hall for a change would go.

16. Whenever impatient duns came after
    Their money, they were sent off with laughter,
        Or else in counterfeit money were paid,
        And very angry and foolish made.

17. His books and clothes he'd sell to pawnbrokers
    And spend the money with drinkers and smokers,
        In short there **was** none of his time could be
        Compared with him in deviltry.

18. To be sure he was often shut up in the Carcer,
    And there to the law was made to answer,
        And for his crimes on one occasion
        He barely escaped the relegation.

19. For three years long he had pursued this vocation,
    And often for money had made application
        To his parents, but his letters were worded so
        That they never suspected their son was such a **go.**

20. That no one in this could poffibly be apter
    Than Hieronimus we fhall fhow in the next chapter,
        Which gives of this queer correfpondence a tafte,
        And therefore now clofe the prefent in hafte.

NOTES.

Stanza 7. *In Floribus*, equivalent to our "living in clover."

Stanza 8. "Let us then rejoice while our youth is blooming!"

Stanza 11. *Pereat*! is the oppofite of *Vivat*!

Stanza 14. *Foxes* are frefhmen.

Stanza 18. The Carcer is the college prison. *Relegation* is difmiffal.

CHAPTER XIV.

Contains the copy of a letter, which, among many others,
the student Hieronimus did write to his parents

D EAR and Honored Parents,
    I lately
Have fuffered for want of money greatly;
  Have the goodnefs, then, to fend without fail
  A trifle or two by return of mail.

2. I want about twenty or thirty ducats;
    For I have not at prefent a cent in my pockets;
        Things are fo tight with us this way,
        Send me the money at once, I pray.

3. And everything is growing higher,
    Lodging and wafhing and lights and fire,
        And incidental expenfes every day—
        Send me the ducats without delay.

4. You can hardly conceive the enormous expenfes
    The college impofes, on all pretences,
        For text-books and lectures fo much to pay—
        I wifh the ducats were on their way!

5. I devote to my ftudies unremitting attention—
    One thing I muft not forget to mention:
        The thirty ducats—pray fend them ftraight
        For my purfe is in a beggarly ftate.

6. Boots and fhoes, and ftockings and breeches,
    Tailoring, wafhing, and extra ftitches,
        Pen, ink and paper, are all fo dear!
        I wifh the thirty ducats were here!

7. The money—(I truft you will fpeedily fend it!)
    I promise faithfully to fpend it;
        Yes, dear parents, you never need fear,
        I live very ftriЄtly and frugally here.

8. When other ftudents revel and riot,
    I fteal away into perfeЄt quiet,
        And fhut myfelf up with my books and light
        In my ftudy-chamber till late at night.

9. Beyond the needful fupply of my table,
   I fpare, dear parents, all I am able;
    Take tea but rarely, and nothing more,
    For fpending money afflicts me fore.

10. Other ftudents, who'd fain be called *mellow*,
    Set me down for a niggardly fellow,
     And fay: there goes the *dig*, juft look!
     How like a parfon he eyes his book!

11. With jibes and jokes they daily befet me,
    But none of thefe things do I fuffer to fret me;
     I fmile at all they can do or fay—
     Don't forget the ducats, I pray!

12. Ten hours each day I fpend at the college,
    Drinking at the fount of knowledge,
     And when the Lectures come to an end,
     The reft in private ftudy I fpend.

13. The Profeffors exprefs great gratification,
    Only they hope I will ufe moderation,
     And not wear out in my ftudiis
     Philofophicis et theologicis.

14. It would favor, dear parents, of felf-laudation,
    To enter on an enumeration
     Of all my ftudies—in brief, there is none
     More exemplary than your dear fon.

15. My head feems ready to burft afunder,
    Sometimes, with its learned load, and I wonder
     Where fo much knowledge is packed away:
     (Apropos! don't forget the ducats, I pray!)

16. Yes, deareſt parents, my devotion to ſtudy
    Conſumes the beſt ſtrength of mind and body,
    And generally even the night is ſpent
    In meditation deep and intent.

17. In the pulpit ſoon I ſhall take my ſtation,
    And try my hand at the preacher's vocation,
    Likewiſe I diſpute in the college-hall
    On learned ſubjects with one and all.

18. But don't forget to ſend me the ducats,
    For I long ſo much to repleniſh my pockets;
    The money, one day ſhall be returned
    In the ſhape of a ſon right wiſe and learn'd.

19. Then my *Privatiſſimum* (I've been thinking on it
    For a long time—and in fact begun it)
    Will coſt me twenty Rix-dollars more,
    Pleaſe ſend with the ducats I mentioned before.

20. I alſo, dear parents, inform you ſadly,
    I have torn my coat of late, very badly,
    So pleaſe encloſe with the reſt in your note
    Twelve dollars to purchaſe a new coat.

21. New boots are alſo neceſſary,
    Likewiſe my night-gown is ragged, very;
    My hat and pantaloons, too, alas!
    And the reſt of my clothes are going to graſs.

22. Now, as all theſe things are needed greatly,
    Pleaſe encloſe me four Louis d'ors ſeparately,
    Which, joined to the reſt, perhaps will be
    Enough for the preſent emergency.

23. My recent ficknefs you may not have heard of,
     In fact, for fome time, my life was defpaired of,
        But I hafte to affure you, on my word,
        That now **my** health is nearly reftored.

24. The Medicus, for fervices rendered,
     A bill of eighteen guilders has tendered,
        And then the apothecary's **will be,**
        In round numbers, about twenty-three.

25. Now that phyfician and apothecary
     May get their dues, it is neceffary
        Thefe forty-one guilders be **added to the** reft,
        But, as to my health, **don't be diftreffed.**

26. The nurfe would alfo **have fome compenfation,**
     Who attended me in my critical fituation,
        I, therefore, think it would be **beft**
        To enclofe feven guilders for **her with** the reft.

27. For citrons, jellies and **things of that nature,**
     To fuftain and ftrengthen the **feeble creature,**
        The confectioner, **too, has a fmall account,**
        Eight guilders is **about the amount.**

28. Thefe various items, of **which I've made mention,**
     Demand immediate **attention ;**
        For order, to me, is **very dear,**
        And I carefully from **debts keep clear.**

29. I alfo rely on your kind **attention,**
     To forward the **ducats of which** I made mention
        So foon as it can poffibly be—
        One more fmall item occurs to me :—

30. Two weeks ago I unluckily ſtumbled,
    And down the length of the ſtairway tumbled,
    　As in at the college door I went,
    　Whereby my right arm almoſt double was bent.

31. The Chirurgus who attended on the occaſion,
    For his balſams, plaſters and preparation
    　Of ſpirits, and other things needleſs to name,
    　Charges 12 dollars; pleaſe forward the ſame.

32. But, that your minds may be acquieſcent,
    I am, thank God, now convaleſcent;
    　Both ſhoulder and ſhin are in a very good way,
    　And I go to lecture every day.

33. My ſtomach is ſtill in a feeble condition,
    A circnmſtance owing, ſo thinks the phyſician,
    　To ſitting ſo much, when I read and write,
    　And ſtudying ſo long and ſo late at night.

34. He, therefore, earneſtly adviſes
    Burgundy wine, with nutmeg and ſpices,
    　And every morning, inſtead of tea,
    　For the ſtomach's ſake to drink ſangaree.

35. Pleaſe ſend, agreeably to theſe advices,
    Two piſtoles for the wine and ſpices,
    　And be ſure, dear parents, I only take
    　Such things as theſe for the ſtomach's ſake.

36. Finally, a few ſmall debts, amounting
    To thirty or forty guilders (looſe counting),
    　Be pleaſed, in your letter, without fail,
    　Dear parents, to encloſe this bagatelle.

37. And could you, for fundries, fend me twenty
   Or a dozen Louis d'or (that would be plenty),
      'Twould be a kindnefs feafonably done,
      And very acceptable to your fon.

38. This letter, dear **parents, comes hoping to find you**
   In ufual health—I beg to remind you
      How much I am for money perplexed,
      Pleafe, therefore, to remit in your next.

39. Herewith I clofe my letter, repeating
   To you and all my friendly greeting,
      And fubfcribe myfelf, without further fufs,
         Your **obedient fon,**
                              HIERONIMUS.

40. I add in a poftfcript what I neglected
   To fay, beloved and highly refpected
      Parents, I beg moft filially,
      That you'll forward the money as foon **as may be.**

41. For I had, dear father (I fay it weeping),
   Fourteen French Crowns laid by in fafe keeping
      (As I thought) for a day of need—but the whole
      An anonymous perfon yefterday ftole.

42. I know you'll make good, unafked, each fhilling,
   Your innocent fon has loft by this villain ;
      For a man fo confiderate muft be aware
      That I fuch a lofs can nowife bear.

43. Meanwhile I'll take care that, to-day or to-morrow,
    Mifter Anonymous fhall, to his forrow
      And your fatisfaction, receive the reward
      Of his gracelefs trick with the hempen cord.

Note.

Stanza 19.   In college, purfuing an extra ftudy with fome Tutor is called taking a *private;* of courfe a *privatiſſmum* would be a *very* private courfe.   See "College Words and cuftoms."

CHAPTER XV.

Here follows a copy of the written reply of old Senator
Jobs to the foregoing letter.

OLD Senator Jobs's anfwer (*verbatim,*
Literatim atque punctatim)
　　In form and manner as follows would run:
　　Dearly beloved and hopeful fon!

2. I am very happy to fee, by thy letter,
　　That thy health and profpects are daily better,
　　　Neverthelefs it caufes me pain,
　　　That thou makeft mention of money again.

3. It is fcarce three months, O **rareft of fcholars!**
　　Since I fent thee a hundred and **fifty dollars,**
　　　I wonder, my fon, thou confidereft **not**
　　　Where in the world fo much **cafh can be got.**

4. I alfo learn, with lively fatisfaction,
　　That thou findeft in ftudy fuch great attraction,
　　　But it is with the higheft concern I fee
　　　That thou afkeft thirty ducats of me.

5. Allow me, **my fon,** the obfervation,
　　That, on the moft liberal computation,
　　　A univerfity refidence
　　　Cannot be, with frugality, fuch an expenfe.

6. Moſt truly thou art right in ſaying
That lectures and books are not had without paying,
But it muſt take a great many to come
To ſuch an enormons, unheard-of ſum.

7. For lodging and waſhing and lights and fire
One cannot poſſibly require
So much, and for paper and pens and ink
A very few pence would ſuffice, I ſhould think.

8. I alſo perceive with gratification
That thou keepeſt thyſelf from the contamination
Of evil companions, eſpecially by night,
Thy books and chamber thy ſole delight.

9. Likewise I am greatly pleaſed with thy drinking
Nothing but tea,—but I can't help thinking:
To one who pores over his books and drinks tea,
What uſe can theſe thirty ducats be?

10. That other ſtudents for a niggard abuſe thee
May very properly amuſe thee,
For he who ſpends all that thou haſt figured,
Deſerves to be called anything but a niggard.

11. Let me adviſe thee to continue the attention
To thy ſtudies of which thou makeſt mention,
That thy precious time and thy money, both,
May be wiſely ſpent and not waſted in ſloth.

12. But mind, my ſon, the advice of the phyſician,
And beware of even a *laudable* ambition,
For alas! too often we find it a rule
That the greateſt ſcholar's the greateſt fool.

13. Thy purpose of preaching deferves commendation,
    Be diligent, therefore, in thy preparation,
        But from much difputation, when all is done,
        Precious little wifdom comes out, my fon.

14. The ufe of a *Privatissimum* I can't conjecture,
    When one is already ten hours at lecture,
        And I comprehend it the lefs, as you fay,
        There are twenty Rixdollars to pay.

15. But I waive all further commentary,
    For the money thou findeft neceffary
        In purfuing thy ftudies I gladly allow,
        And though it were three times as much as now.

16. According to thy ftory (no doubt a true one),
    Thou haft torn thy coat, and need'ft a new one,
        Neverthelefs the cloth muft be fuperfine,
        To coft twelve dollars, or even nine.

17. But he that will ftudy to be a paftor,
    Should not drefs fo much better than his Mafter,
        Therefore a fomewhat coarfer ftuff
        Would make thee a coat quite good enough.

18. For other articles of wearing apparel
    About the four Louis d'or, I shan't quarrel,
        When night-gown, hat and trowfers wear out,
        New ones are neceffary without doubt.

19. But if I muft make, for all this raiment,
    And fo forth, fpecial and feparate payment,
        What fhall become, Hieronimus dear,
        Of the thirty ducats, to me is not clear.

20. I received with much feeling the information
    Of thy recent critical fituation,
        But to tamper with phyfic to fuch an extent,
        I muft fay, my fon, is money mifpent.

21. For I fcarce ever knew of the rule failing,
    With young folks efpecially, that when one is ailing,
        Nature does better when left to herfelf,
        Than the beft mixture on the apothecary's fhelf.

22. The expenfe of the Doctor and his preparation
    Seems to me little lefs than an abomination,
        And I very ferioufly queftion :
        Can an apothecary or a Doctor be a Chriftian ?

23. And as to the nurfe's compenfation
    Who attended you in your critical fituation,
        'Twould have been enough if thou hadft given
        A fingle guilder inftead of feven.

24. Unlefs fhe had previoufly fhown thee attention
    Of another defcription which thou doft not mention,
        For this, dear fon, I am forced to infer,
        From thy paying feven guilders to her.

25. And then the confectioner's bill of eight guilders—
    My fon, my fon ! it almoft bewilders
        Thy father's brain !—if thou hadft been wife,
        A dollar at moft would now fuffice.

26. For citrons, confits, and things of that nature,
    Adminifter no ftrength to the feeble creature,
        But oatmeal gruel and barley drinks
        Are better, far, for the fick, methinks.

27. To fall down ftairs is highly injurious,
   See to it next time thou art not fo furious
       To get to thy ftudies, but take more care,
       For it cofts a great deal fuch damage to repair.

28. Thy furgeon has taken thee in completely,
   For our town-barber, who works fo neatly,
       Will, for twelve dollars, I'm told, reftore
       A broken leg as whole as before.

29. But I'm happy to hear of thy reftoration,
   For when the parfon is in his peroration,
       His arm muft be in a flexible ftate,
       That fo he may pound and gefticulate.

30. I muft further lament thy ftomach's weaknefs
   Occafioned by thy recent ficknefs;
       My ftomach, I'm forry to fay, is feeble
       From fitting fo much at the Council-table.

31. Neverthelefs my earneft advice is:
   Abftain from Burgundy wine and fpices;
       A bit of flag-root now and then
       Will help thy ftomach as much again.

32. Thou mentioneft "fome fmall debts, amounting
   To thirty or forty guilders, (loofe counting);"
       I've thought and thought and racked my brain
       To guefs what debts thofe can be, but in vain.

33. Thou haft given already in fpecification,
   Item by item (outfide calculation),
       And forty guilders, thou knoweft full well,
       Upon my foul are no "bagatelle!"

34. And finally thou needeſt (for ſuch thy pretence is),
    A dozen Piſtoles for thy general expenſes;
      No doubt it were very agreeable to thee,
      But to me inconvenient in the higheſt degree.

35. For as to any unexpected urgency
    Thoſe *thirty ducats* will meet the emergency,
      Theſe laſt dozen Louis d'or ſeem to me,
      In that view, a mere ſuperfluity.

36. And as to the ſtolen crowns, thy ſuggeſtion,
    In point of delicacy, admits of a queſtion,
      For truly the reparation were ſorer to me
      Than the alleged robbery is to thee.

37. But, from this diſagreeable ſubjeƈt to paſs on,
    Thy propoſal to ſtring the thief up ſans façon
      Is by no means a Chriſtian ſentiment;
      Mr. Anonymous may one day repent.

38. Beſides, 'tis a matter of congratulation
    In theſe our days of illumination,
      I ſay it confidentially in thy ear,
      Holy juſtice has grown leſs ſevere.

39. No one who chances a drawer to rifle,
    Need mount the double ladder for ſuch a trifle,
      At leaſt, in our wiſe Schildburg they ſay,
      Far greater rogues go clear every day.

40. When thou in future haſt money in keeping,
    I adviſe thee to guard it with vigilance unſleeping,
      For nothing is ſo univerſal a ſubjeƈt of ſpeculation
      As money depoſited for preſervation.

41. I and thy mother underſtand the thing better,
    Learn wiſdom, therefore, from this preſent letter
    　We always lock our caſh up tight
    　And anxiouſly watch it by day and night.

42. But to appeaſe thy preſent deſire,
    And ſupply what immediate wants require,
    　Be pleaſed hereby the moneys to find
    　In a ſealed linen bag, each ſeparate kind.

43. Neverthelefs, I muſt hint to thee, Hieronimus,
    That the times we live in are rather ominous,
    　And it coſts me many an anxious thought
    　Where ſo much money can ever be got.

44. There's a very ſmall trifle of buſineſs doing,
    Folks are ſo poor—ſcarce anything brewing
    　In the honorable Council, and ſo
    　My incomes, you ſee, are very low.

45. I ſhall, therefore, await with pleaſed expectation,
    The day of thy final graduation,
    　Eſpecially as, by this time, without doubt,
    　Thou haſt in every branch learned out.

46. For if thou ſhould'ſt longer ſtay and ſtudy
    As diligently and *dearly* as thou haſt already,
    　I ſhall grow as poor as Job was once,
    　Utterly unable to raiſe any more funds.

47. We all deſire to welcome, greatly,
    Our learned ſon in a ſtyle right ſtately,
    　Eſpecially thy mother with joy
    　Looks forward to the return of her boy.

48. I wifh I had fome news to write you,
    But things are moftly in *quo fitû*;
      I go as ufual, early and late,
      To the Council-room to deliberate.

49. There we have had in confideration,
    In pleno, many an alteration,
      Whereby our police affairs may be
      Adminiftered judicioufly.

50. Thy mother's teeth have troubled her greatly,
    But a diftinguifhed furgeon, lately,
      From foreign parts, came along one day,
      And took the troublefome teeth away.

51. A perfon is paying attention to your fifter
    Gertrude, his name and title is Mifter
      Procurator Geier, 'tis well under way,
      And Trudy grows taller every day.

52. Our old parfon is always ailing,
    They think his health is decidedly failing,
      If this excellent man fhould be taken away,
      Thou mighteft be our Parfon one day.

53. Our wealthy neighbor's daughter Betty
    Sends hearty greetings—the girl is pretty,
      And neat and tidy, and would be
      A nice little parfon's wife for thee.

54. Thy brothers and fifters all fend their greeting
    In the joyful hope of a fpeedy meeting,
      They are glad to hear of thy health and fuccefs,
      And, with wifhes for thy happinefs,

55. I remain,

      Thy father (in courfe of **natur**),

Hans Jobs, *pro tempore* Senater.

   P. S.   Write again **at** an early day,

  But fpare thy allufions to money, I **pray.**

NOTES.

Stanza **40.**   Does not the laft couplet feem **almoft** pro-phetic?

Stanza **43.**   N. B.—The rhyme in the firft couplet is ftrictly copy-righted.

Stanza 48.   The fecond line fhows old **Jobs a rare Latinift.**

Stanza **49.**   In pleno—or, **as** *we* might **fay,** "in Com-mittee **of the** Whole."

CHAPTER XVI.

How Hieronimus finifhed his ftudies, and how he
journeyed home, and how it ftood with his learning;
neatly reprefented in the prefent engraving.

SINCE, now, one cannot forever tarry
At univerfities, it became neceffary
 That after a fpace of three years had flown
 Hieronimus fhould prepare to go home.

2. As his time of ftudy had now fully expired
And his prefence at home was very much defired,
 Immediately he fet about
 Doing all that was needed to fit himfelf out.

3. His luggage required but a fhort time to pack it
   For faving boots, fword, waiftcoat and jacket,
     And whatever elfe on his body was feen,
     There was no other article, dirty or clean.

4. For books there was no need of afking about them,
   He could get along very well without them,
     And except a fingle fermon alone
     Not the leaft fcripture did he own.

5. A friend had given him this as a prefent,
   And taught him to repeat it by labour inceffant,
     That fo, whenever an occafion tranfpired,
     He might preach eafily at home if defired.

6. He thought with no little trepidation
   Of prefenting himfelf to his parents in this fituation,
     For if in this manner he fhould appear,
     The ftate of the cafe would at once be clear.

7. At laft he concluded, that when they began to
   Inquire about his purfe and portmanteau,
     He would make believe that fomebody ftole,
     On his journey home, the whole.

8. Alfo fome fighs would ftart, quite ominous,
   How will it fare with thee, poor Hieronimus!
     When thou an examination fhalt undergo,
     And fhow how much thou doft not know?

9. Verily he was filled with remorfe and vexation
   So that he almoft fhed tears on the occafion,
     To think that for fo much time and coft
     He had fo little learning to boaft.

10. But all his manœuvering, contriving and inventing,
    Wifhing and fighing and groaning and grunting,
      Brought him no fort of peace at all,
      For the time was gone beyond recall.

11. Therefore, by way of alleviation,
    He fent out formaliter an invitation
      To his friends at the univerfity,
      And gave them a valedictory fpree.

12. Here then, once more, was a regular rollicking,
    Drinking and fmoking and finging and frolicking,
      'Till at laft the difmal morning breaks,
      And Hieronimus his farewell takes.

13. Right heavily now his heart was fhaken
    And bitter grief did the parting awaken,
      Yes, he really boohoo'd right out
      In the arms of the friends that crowded about.

14. Before, however, his final clearance,
    At the Profeffor's he made his appearance,
      Who gave him, for the ready money,
      An academic teftimony.

15. It was not indeed quite creditable,
    But Hieronimus, who to read it was unable,
      (For it was written in Latin and Greek)
      Into his bag the paper did ftick.

16. We leave him, therefore, his journey purfuing
    Homeward, the reader meanwhile may be viewing,
      Prefixed to this chapter, a copper-plate
      That fhows, as to learning, his real ftate.

CHAPTER XVII.

How Hieronimus, booted and spurred, returns to his friends.

ONE day when old Senator Jobs, after dinner,
(For such was his accustomed manner,)
 With pipe in mouth, leaned back his head
 In the easy-chair and his newspaper read;

2. And meanwhile, Mrs. Jobs was making a pother
In the kitchen, about something or other,
 And nobody dreaming of any harm,
 All on a sudden there rose an alarm;

3. For a ſtately rider, booted and ſpurry,
   Came riding up the ſtreet in a hurry,
       And ſtraight at the houſe they heard, ſlam-bang,
       Somebody diſmount with a terrible clang.

4. Like a knell in the family's ears it ſounded,
   Old Jobs let fall his paper, aſtounded,
       And the pipe itſelf came near to break;
       And Mrs. Jobs was too frightened to ſpeak.

5. But ſoon from this panic in which they were taken,
   The rider did their ſenſes 'waken,
       As, in full traveling coſtume,
       He came at once right into the room.

6. The old folks apparently neither of them knew him,
   But he kept quiet and let them view him,
       Till at laſt the old man jumped from his chair
       To ſee his dear Hieronimus there.

7. I have not the qualifications in any meaſure,
   To ſing the exceeding and mighty pleaſure
       Of the good old Senator at ſeeing his boy,
       He almoſt went out of his head for joy.

8. The mother too, could hardly contain herſelf,
   Nor from kiſſing his hands and feet reſtrain herſelf,
       As ſoon as ſhe ſaw that it muſt needs be
       Hieronimus, and none but he.

9. They almoſt cried, in the overmeaſure
   Of their very great and diſtreſſing pleaſure,
       And the Welcome home! and the God be praiſed!
       Held on till a ſtranger had been half-crazed.

10. And Senator Jobs's remaining children
 Were alfo at hand, till it became quite bewilderin',
  They all of them feemed in a perfect bother,
  For not a foul of them knew their brother.

11. 'Twas really exceeding curious
 To hear what the children made of Hieronimus:
  One held him to be a diftinguifhed gueft
  Who had juft arrived from the Eaft or Weft;

12. Another, on account of his fword and his danger-
 ous drefs and equipment, confidered the ftranger
  As one who bags up children fmall;
  This thought did the youngeft particularly appal.

13. **But** very funny was it with Efther,
 Our Hieronimus's youngeft fifter,
  For fhe kept up a continual clack
  About her ftrange uncle from Gengenbach.

14. In the three years he had fpent at college,
 His perfon had quite outgrown their knowledge,
  His belly had waxed exceeding thick
  And there was a deal of hair on chin and cheek.

15. It was not, therefore, **a matter of wonder**
 That they at firft fhould make fuch a blunder,
  Efpecially as his ftudent-drefs
  Made it difficult, who he was, to guefs.

16. A **very** tall hat with a very tall feather,
 Breeches and waiftcoat of yellow buck's leather,
  With a fhort cravat of fome gray ftuff,
  Difguifed Hieronimus well enough.

17. Add to this a mighty great fword, fufpended
    From his left fide, with which he defended
       His perfon from any fudden attack,
       Fit alike for a thruft or a thwack.

18. And then his look, fo martial and bloody,
    That feemed to threaten death to everybody ;
       His hair hanging down in great maffes too,
       And behind, a great pig-tail of a queue.

19. Thefe and other arrangements I might mention,
    Soon attracted his father's attention,
       For a fimple decorous black drefs
       Would better have fuited his parents, I guefs.

20. Nor did Hieronimus's general behaviour
    Recommend him to old father Jobs's favour,
       Efpecially when he Hieronimus heard
       Venting curfes at every word.

21. He gave him, therefore, to underftand clearly
    That he muft alter all this entirely,
       For furely a young Theologus
       Muft never be heard to fwear and cufs.

22. When a few moments after he afked for the coffer,
    Hieronimus did the information proffer,
       And fwore to it moft luftily :
       It was ftolen from the poftwagon, faid he.

23. This difagreeable information
    Threw the father into great agitation,
       And he would immediately have begun
       To fcold, but the mother excufed her fon ;

24. Sne ftepped between Hieronimus and his father,
Saying, 'tis furely the misfortune rather
 Than any fault of our dear fon ;
 So the old man fubmitted and was mum.

25. Meanwhile the neighbours were rapidly learning
The news of Hieronimus's returning,
 From houfe to houfe the rumour flew
 'Till it was known the whole town through.

26. It feemed a weighty public matter,
It kept the ftreets in a conftant clatter,
 And at every cafual neighborly meeting
 " Hieronimus is here " was the very firft greeting.

27. In univerfal congratulation,
At Senator Jobs's habitation,
 The reft of the remaining day did wag
 And nothing more was thought of the bag.

28. Hieronimus feafted away quite cheery,
For his journey had made him faint and weary,
 And he fmoked till he emptied, as I can vouch,
 His daddy's great tobacco pouch.

NOTE.

In the wood-cut that heads this Chapter, the object on the left refembling a fcrew, as if to draw the rider along by an invifible wire, is prefumed to be no more nor lefs than a mile-ftone. The reader will pleafe not let it difturb his dreams.

f

CHAPTER XVIII.

How Hieronimus now began to be clerical, and how he
got a black drefs and a peruke, and how he preached
for the firft time in the pulpit, &c.

THE day after that to which we've been referring,
When all in the houfe were up and ftirring,
    And round the breakfaft table they fat,
    Sipping their coffee in focial chat,

2. The father began to call attention
    As follows : Dear Son, it is proper to mention,
        That thy ftyle of raiment hitherto
        Will for the future hardly do.

3. And firft and foremoft muft thou haften
    That terrible fword from thy fide to unfaften,
        Becaufe a fervant of the Lord
        Don't never fight except with the word.

4. Likewife the gray collar and waiftcoat of leather
    And breeches and boots muft be laid afide altogether,
        As alfo the mighty feather hat,
        For no clergyman is allowed to wear that.

5. For if this rig fhould be feen by any body,
   They would certainly cry out, "O **Luddy!**
      We've furely got a cuiraffier,
      Inftead of our future parfon, here."

6. **Know** alfo that a round peruke is fitter
   For a clerical head and looks much better,
      And a great deal more refpectable, too,
      Than ropy hair and a pig-tail queue!

7. It is therefore thy father's pleafure
   That the tailor fhould come and take thy meafure,
      That he may make thee this very day
      A fuit of black without delay.

8. **The peruke-maker has alfo had warning,**
   To come, if you pleafe, this very morning,
      To make thee a wig that thou mayft wear
      Over thy frowzy head of hair.

9. It will make thee look refpectable, very,
   But it is alfo neceffary
      That thou fhouldft leave off fwearing to-day
      And endeavour to live in a clerical way.

10. Hieronimus liftened, reluctantly rather,
    To the rational counfel of his father,
       But concluded to fulfil the defire
       Of his grave and venerable fire.

11. Behold him, therefore, ere the day had expired,
    In full black drefs and peruke attired,
       He was alfo in a white cravat arrayed
       By his mother's *manu propriâ* made.

12. Thus clerically fitted out, he communicated
    To his parents that he meditated,
    God willing, in this livery
    To preach next Sunday publicly.

13. On the Sunday following Hieron'mus
    Did really preach in purfuance of his promife,
    And without fpecial obftacle
    Got through his fermon very well.

14. For as we above, Chapter XVI., made mention,
    A friend had politely fhown him the attention
    Of writing for him a fermon, which he
    Could now deliver conveniently.

15. 'Twas an excellent piece of compofition,
    Choke full of wifdom and erudition,
    And fmelt fo of the ftudy fhelf
    That Hieronimus did'nt underftand it himfelf.

16. His external appearance was likewife fplendid,
    His arms and hands he mightily extended,
    And his tenor voice fo ftrong and clear
    Went ftately into the public ear.

17. His fermon was heard by many hundred,
    Who all at his talent greatly wondered,
    They nodded their heads and the whifper ran
    Through all the houfe: "What a wonderful man!

18. "Who on earth would have ever fufpected
    That anything like this could have been concocted
    Out of Jobs's dull Hieronimus?
    'Tis a perfect miracle to us!"

19. Likewife there was not a fingle **relation**
    Abfent from the congregation,
    > And every one thought: "Our coufin Jobs
    > **Looks** remarkably well in his clerical robes!"

20. But 'tis vain to attempt to defcribe the elation
    Of the two good parents on this occafion,
    > There cannot be a doubt, thought they,
    > **He's** the greateft orator of the day.

21. When divine fervice had come to a termination,
    They adjourned to partake of a great collation,
    > Given in Senator Jobs's houfe,
    > **Where** all the relations went to caroufe.

22. **And while the dinner they were eating,**
    Hieronimus' praife they were conftantly repeating,
    > And many a great glafs of wine
    > Was drunk to the health of our young divine.

23. The whole affembly was alfo unanimous
    That, under exifting circumftances, Hieronimus,
    > Who to-day had preached fo brilliantly
    > **Before the prefent company,**

24. **Muft** certainly next make bold to venture
    His name as candidate to **enter,**
    > That fo, in optima formâ he
    > Should Candidatus Minifterii be.

25. **'Tis true, as a preliminary,**
    An Examen would be neceffary,
    > But the recent fpecimen fhowed that he
    > **Would** find therein no difficulty.

26. Especially as the present incumbent was weakly,
    Old and infirm and somewhat sickly,
      Hieronimus might without any offence
      Enter the vacant parish at once.

27. That is, in case, by the blessing of heaven,
    The parson should go the way of all living,
      For his feeble constitution gave place
      For suspicion that this would be shortly the case.

28. Hieronimus, overpowered by the solicitations
    And weighty reasons of his friends and relations,
      Gave, anxiously enough, God knows,
      His consent to what they did propose.

29. For the rest, he emptied with great pleasure
    Of liquor many a brimming measure,
      But when that Examen came into his head
      It struck his heart with a sort of dread.

30. At last his anxiety sought consolation
    In a regular fit of intoxication,
      Although old Jobs his displeasure made known,
      By repeatedly shaking his head at his son.

Note.

Stanza 8. *Frowzy.* This word is not *frouzy*, which has a different meaning. Our word is found only in an old Dictionary in the Jobs family.

CHAPTER XIX.

How Hieronimus was examined for a Candidate, and how he made out.

HOWEVER he ſtuck to his determination,
And the clerify held a convocation,
 And every one came in his wig and robes
 To the examination of Hieronimus Jobs.

2. But how he felt in view of his danger,
Being to learning an utter ſtranger,
 And what an anxious face he made,
 The reader will not comprehend, I'm afraid.

3. The ſcene is beyond my power of painting:
If he ever in his life ſaw the hour for fainting,
 That hour at laſt was approaching now;
 Alas! thou poor Hieronimus, thou!

4. Begin now, Miſs Muſe, an enumeration
Of the clerical gentleman whom the examination
 Brought hither on the appointed day
 From every quarter of Swabia.

5. The firſt, *that* was the *Herr Inſpector*,
   In doctrine ſtrong as a ſecond Hector,
   A ſtately, pot-bellied man was he,
   Whom you ſaw at a glance an Inſpector to be.

6. This poſt was accorded to his ſingular merit,
   Its burdens he bore with a patient ſpirit,
   And, to ſay the truth, with a cheerful mood,
   And daily ate and drank what was good.

7. And after him came the *ghoſtly Aſſeſſor*,
   A man whoſe breadth was ſomewhat leſſer,
   But height much greater: he was ſpare of limb,
   And his diſpoſition exceedingly grim.

8. He not only the ſpiritual intereſts defended,
   But to matters of economy alſo attended,
   And drank only bad wine and beer,
   For his income was ſmall and his habit ſevere.

9. Then came *Herr Krager*, an oldiſh man rather,
   Who was very well verſed in many a church father,
   And to prove a point could readily quote
   Whatever any one of 'em wrote.

10. Next *Herr Kriſch*, polite as a Caſtilian,
    Who was, in Poſtils, a perfect poſtillion;
    Poſted up in them as well as the beſt
    Parſon the Swabian land poſſeſſed.

11. Next *Herr Beff*, a Linguiſt of great reputation,
    And a tolerable chriſtian in walk and converſation,
    In lecturing a terrible bore,
    But always Orthodox to the core.

12. Next *Herr Schrei*, a man of great notoriety
    Alike in the pulpit and in general fociety,
        Free and eafy—had no wife,
        And led with his cook an exemplary life.

13. Next *Herr Plotz*, an angelic creature,
    In his youth of a fomewhat genial nature,
        But when to preach he once began
        He became a very pious man.

14. He kept his belovéd congregation
    From vice and evil communication,
        Faithful in feafon and out was he
        To admonifh, when he had opportunity.

15. Next *Herr Keffer*, who never could tire
    In following his fheep through mud and mire,
        But alas! in his flock, befide the lambs,
        Were likewife many ftiff-necked old rams.

16. Sometimes, to get them to follow his leadings,
    He inftituted legal proceedings,
        For he underftood the jura of the ftate
        As well as the very beft advocate.

17. Befides thofe named in the above enumeration,
    Other clerical gentlemen attended the examination,
        Whom I neither need nor can
        Particularly defignate man by man.

18. Now when the reverend and ghoftly faces
    Had all come together in their places,
        Præmiffis præmittendis, they
        Round a great table fate ftraightway.

19. With trembling and quaking came Hieronimus
Before this affembly of white bands fo ominous,
    And fcraped a greeting fubmiffively,
    Oh, woe, Hieronimus! woe on thee!

20. Firft and formoft inquired the *Examinatores*
About his previous manners and *mores*,
    And prefently afked him whether he
    Had a certificate from the univerfity?

21. Hieronimus, without hefitation,
Handed the infpector the atteftation,
    Who read the fame immediately:
    Alas! Hieronimus, woe on thee!.

22. 'Tis true, the document was worded,
In Latin and Greek, as above recorded,
    And confequently not eafy to read,
    But unfortunately, as ill luck decreed,

23. The Infpector made out, in a free tranflation
To give a fubftantial interpretation,
    For no other clergyman in the hall
    Dared undertake the tafk at all.

24. **To leave no breach** in this narration,
I will now give the reader full information,
    What Hieronimus' certificate,
    Word for word, did properly ftate.

25. Firft the name and title of the Profeffors,
And then in larger hand, the letters
    L. B. S., and the meaning of them
    Was *Lectori Benevolo Salutem!*

26. "Forafmuch as Herr Hieronimus Jobsius
     As Theologiæ Studiofus,
        During three years' and fome weeks' fpace
        Had his refidence in this place,—

27. "And the fame now has it in contemplation
     To take his leave, and has made application
        For a written certificate to me,
        A ftep of great propriety,—

28. "I could not refufe his reafonable defires,
     But give hereby the atteft he requires,
        That the fame did every quarter of a year
        Once at my lecture-room appear.

29. "Whether the reft was devoted to ftudy
     Himfelf knows better than anybody,
        For I in this official report
        Affert and teftify nothing of the fort.

30. "And as to general behaviour,
     There is not much to be faid in his favour,
        Entire filence on that point would be
        The part of chriftian charity.

31. "For the reft I have only to fay, God fpeed him
     On his journey home, and may heaven lead him,
        When all thefe earthly troubles are paft,
        To the place where he belongs at laft!"

32. How the eyes of the learned body diftended
     When the reading of this document ended,
        And that Herr Hieronimus did not laugh
        The reader can imagine readily enough.

33. However on all hands it feemed better
    For this once to overlook the matter,
      And for charity's fake to find all the good
      In the teftimonial that they could.

34. For the gentlemen wifely recollected
    How many of *their* tricks had not been detected,
      And how if they had, it had fared with them,
      And fo they proceeded at once *ad rem.*

35. The Herr Infpector he led off,
    Clearing the way with a mighty cough,
      Repeated thrice, thrice did he ftroke
      His portly paunch and then he fpoke:

36. "I, for the time *pro tempore* Infpector
    And of the clergy prefent Director,
      Afk you: *Quid fit Epifcopus?*"
      Straightway replied Hieronimus:

37. "A Bifhop is, as I conjecture,
    An altogether agreeable mixture
      Of fugar, pomegranate juice and red wine,
      And for warming and ftrengthening very fine."

38. The Candidate Jobs this anfwer making,
    There followed of heads a general fhaking!
      And firft the Infpector faid, hem! hem!
      Then the others *fecundum ordinem.*

39. And now the *Affeffor* began to inquire:
    "*Herr Hieronimus! tell me, I defire,*
      Who the Apoftles may have been?"
      Hieronimus quick made anfwer again:

40. "Apoſtles they call great jugs, I'm thinking,
    In which wine and beer are kept for drinking,
      In the villages, and from them oft
      By thirſty Burſches liquor is quaffed."

41. The Candidate Jobs this anſwer making,
    There followed of heads a general ſhaking,
      And firſt the Inſpector ſaid, hem! hem!
      Then the others *ſecundum ordinem.*

42. Herr Krager now in his turn ſtood ready:
    And "*if you pleaſe, Herr Candidate,*" ſaid he,
      "*Inform me who was St. Auguſtin?*"
      Hieronimus anſwered with open mien:

43. "The only Auguſtine of whom I've any knowledge
    Is the one I uſed to know at college,
      Auguſtine, the beadle of the univerſity,
      Who often before the Prorector cited me."

44. The Candidate Jobs this anſwer making,
    There followed of heads a general ſhaking,
      And firſt the Inſpector ſaid hem! hem!
      Then the others *ſecundum ordinem.*

45. Now followed Herr Kriſch at once and requeſted
    To know "*of how many parts a ſermon conſiſted,*
      In other words, how many diviſions muſt there be,
      When it is written ruleably?" ſaid he.

46. Hieronimus having taken a moment to determine,
    Replied; "There are two parts to every ſermon:
      The one of theſe two parts no man
      Can underſtand, but the other he can."

8

47. The Candidate Jobs this anfwer making,
    There followed of heads a general fhaking,
    And firft the Infpector faid hem! hem!
    Then the others *fecundum ordinem.*

48. Herr Beff the Linguift continued the examination,
    And defired of Herr Hieronimus information:
    " *What the Hebrew Kibbutz might be ?*"
    Hieronimus's anfwer was fomewhat free:

49. " I find in a book to which I've paid attention,
    Sophia's tour from Memel to Saxony, mention,
    That fhe to the furly Kibbutz fell
    Becaufe fhe refufed the rich old fwell."

50. The Candidate Jobs this anfwer making,
    There followed of heads a general fhaking,
    And firft the Infpector faid hem! hem!
    Then the others *fecundum ordinem.*

51. Next in turn it came to Herr Schreier,
    Who did of Hieronimus inquire,
    " *How many claffes of angels he*
    Confidered there might properly be ?"

52. Hieronimus anfwered, " He never pretended
    With all the angels to be acquainted,
    But there was one of them he knew
    On the Angel-Tavern fign, painted blue."

53. The Candidate Jobs this anfwer making,
    There followed of heads a general fhaking,
    And firft the Infpector faid hem! hem!
    And the others *fecundum ordinem.*

54. Herr Plotz proceeded with the interrogation :
   " *Can you give, Herr Candidate, an enumeration*
   Of the concilia æcumenica ?"
   And Hieronimus anfwered ! " Sir,

55. " When I at the univerfity did ftudy
   I was often cited before a body
   Called a council, but it never feemed to me
   To have anything to do with economy."

56. The Candidate Jobs this anfwer making,
   There followed of heads a general fhaking,
   And firft the Infpector faid, hem ! hem !
   Then the others *fecundum ordinem.*

57. Then followed his fpiritual lordfhip, Herr Keffer,
   The queftion he ftarted feemed fomewhat tougher,
   It related " *to the Manichean herefy*
   And what their faith was originally."

58. Anfwer : " Yes thefe fimple devils
   Did really think that without any cavils,
   Before my departure, I fhould pay them off
   And in fact I did cudgel them foundly enough."

59. The Candidate Jobs this anfwer making,
   There followed of heads a general fhaking,
   And firft the Infpector said, hem! hem !
   Then the others *fecundum ordinem.*

60. The remaining queftions that received attention
   For want of room I omit to mention ;
   For otherwife the protocol
   Would exceed feven fheets, if given in full.

61. For there were many queftions, dogmatical,
    Polemical and hermeneutical,
      To which Hieronimus made reply
      In the manner above, fucceffively.

62. And likewife many queftions in philology
    And other fciences ending in *ology*,
      And whatever elfe to a clergyman may
      Be put on examination day.

63. When the Candidate Jobs his anfwer was making,
    There would follow of heads a general fhaking,
      And firft the Infpector would fay hem! hem!
      Then the others, *fecundum ordinem*.

64. Now when the examination had expired,
    Hieronimus by permiffion retired,
      That the cafe might be viewed on every fide,
      And the council carefully decide:

65. If concience would advife the admiffion
    Of Hieronimus to the pofition
      And clafs of candidates for the
      Holy Gofpel miniftry.

66. Immediately they proceeded to voting,
    But very foon, without much difputing,
      The meeting was unanimous
      That, under the circumftances, Hieronimus

67. Would not perfift in his application
    As a candidate for ordination,
      But for fpecial reafons they thought it beft,
      To let the matter quietly reft.

68. In fact for years it was kept fo private,
    No ftranger ever heard anything of it,
      But everybody early and late
      Held Hieronimus for a candidate.

NOTES.

Stanza 48. *Kibbutz* is a corruption for the Hebrew letter Koph.

Stanza 49. Kibbutz is alfo a name for the Owl.

Stanza 57. The German ftudents nickname their creditors *Manichæans*.

CHAPTER XX.

How the author submissively begs pardon, that the former
chapter was so long, and how he promises that the
present one shall be so much the shorter; a chapter of
which the rubric is longer than the chapter itself, and
which might be omitted without injuring the story.

I HEARTILY beg the reader's pardon,
The previous chapter was such a long and hard one,
The present chapter, dear reader, shall be
So much the shorter, I promise thee.

CHAPTER XXI.

How Father Jobs the Senator did deliver Hieronimus a
sermon of rebuke, and how he dies of chagrin.

THE reader fhould have feen the confternation
That rofe in Jobs's habitation,
  Becaufe the Examen did not tranfpire
  Entirely in accordance with the general defire.

2. But what then did Hieronimus's father?
Dear reader! pray afk me, **what didn't he** do rather?
  He feized Hieronimus by the nape
  Of the neck, and faid to him, " Thou fcape-

3. " grace! is't for this I fuch kindnefs have done thee
And lavifhed whole handfulls of money upon thee,
  'Till I almoft myfelf a poor man became,
  To reap only mortification and fhame?

4. " Had'ft thou but ftudied with application
And behaved in a manner worthy of approbation,
  Thou wouldft without doubt at this time be
  A Candidatus Minifterii.

5. " And wouldft get a parifh foon and be famous;
But now thou art only an ignoramus,
  Who nothing of theology knows,
  And all his life long breadlefs goes.

6. " Thy mother and I were often expreffing
   Our hopes that thou wouldft be one day a bleffing
    To our old age, but oh, what a cufs
    Thou haft proved, thou vile Hieronimus!

7. " All that thou ufedft to write of thy doing,
   How many ftudies thou waft purfuing,
    And that none in diligence equalled thee,—
    Was a pack of lies, as I now can fee.

8. " And all that was faid of thy privatiffimo
   And about the ten hours in collegio,
    How kind the profeffors were to thee,
    And thy folitary drinking of tea;

9. " Item, of all the various learning
   With which thy head was in danger of turning,
    And thy meditation late at night,
    And of other fimilar things a fight;

10. " And about thy ftomach becoming fo feeble
    By bending over the ftudy table,
     The whole of it, as I now find,
     Was nothing at all but lies and wind.

11. " Oh that I only had liftened in feafon
    To our good Rector's counfel and reafon,
     Who very clearly intimated to me,
     That nothing good could be made of thee.

12. " Then had been fpared a vaft deal of money
    And many a good round patrimony,
     Which thou, good-for-nothing fcoundre!, I fay,
     At the univerfity haft tippled away!"

13. Such, as the fon ftood trembling **before him,**
    Was the fermon with which old Jobs **did fcore him,**
      In fact his anger had rifen fo quick
      That at firft he came near ufing the **ftick.**

14. Meanwhile as fcolding and getting furious
    Is generally to health injurious,
      As might be imagined very well,
      The good old man into a fever fell.

15. In his well days, when younger and tougher,
    Severe attacks of gout he would fuffer,
      His Counfellor's office, good living **and ease**
      Predifpofed him to this difeafe.

16. But now all at once his pains forfook him,
    And in the heart the Podagra took him,
      And after four-and-twenty hours
      He emigrated from this world of ours.

17. No end was there now to the grieving and groaning,
    The houfe all wringing their hands and moaning,
      And even Hieronimus's grief
      Hardly admitted any relief.

18. The reader, I fear, would foon be yawning,
    If I fhould defcribe thefe fcenes of mourning
      Any farther, I therefore ceafe
      And leave poor old Senator Jobs in peace.

CHAPTER XXII.

How Hieronimus almoſt became Tutor to a young Baron.

ALTHOUGH a fortnight had now expired
Since Senator Jobs to his reſt retired,
    The thought of the widow Jobs ſtill ran
    At times on her dear departed man.

2. Hieronimus meanwhile took his fodder
    Up to this time at the houſe of his mother,
        And would gladly in ſuch idleneſs
        Have paſſed his entire life, I gueſs ;

3. Had he not received a propoſition
    To look about for a change in condition,
        Whereby he might, in the time to come,
        Get his living more properly than at home.

4. For it was all over with the expectation
    Of getting, as parſon, a ſituation,
        So ſoon as this moſt heinous dunce
        Had preached in each village his ſermon once

5. Since now many men of great importance
    Began as tutors to make their fortunes,
        It entered into Hieronimus's view
        That he would be tutor ſomewhere, too.

6. And fortune feemed not unpropitious
  To Hieronimus's wifhes,
    For about two months from that time or three
    He heard of a fine opportunity.

7. For a neighboring nobleman, (here namelefs)
  Advertifed for a tutor of character blamelefs,
    Who for low board and 8 guilders fhould come
    And teach the young baron, his only fon.

8. Religion, morality, five kinds of languages
  Reading and writing and fuch like appendages,
    Philofophy, phyfic, geography,
    Arithmetic, hiftory, poetry.

9. Drawing and dancing and riding and fencing
  And other accomplifhments needlefs to mention,
    Thefe were the branches, every one
    To be taught for 8 guilders to the baron's fon.

10. The Candidate Hieronimus was defired
  To call on his grace, who at once inquired,
    Whether the faid Hieronimus was the one
    Who for eight guilders would teach his fon?

11. Hieronimus made anfwer: "Gracious
  "Sir, it is exceedingly vexatious
    To be a tutor, and eight guilders would be
    In my opinion quite a fmall fee;

12. "However to do your grace a pleafure,
  I will at once fall in with the meafure,
    And fee forthwith what can be done,
    In the way of inftructing the baron your fon."

13. And fo was completed the negotiation,
    When, contrary to all expectation,
      One little difficulty occurred,
      Which may be ftated in a word:

14. Whether Hieronimus in the things defired,
    Could undergo the examination required,
      Which he would be obliged to teach every one,
      To the young baron, the nobleman's fon?

15. But it foon appeared indifputable,
    That Hieronimus was not able
      Himfelf, to underftand a fingle one
      Of the things he was to teach the nobleman's fon.

16. He therefore received a quiet difmiffion
    And jogged home again in an unpleafant condition
      Of mind, and vented his curfes upon
      The tutorfhip and the nobleman's fon.

17. His grace now right and left inquired
    Whether another could poffibly be hired,
      Who for the fum of eight guilders would come
      And teach the young baron, his only fon.

18. Whether he has found it in his power
    To obtain fuch a perfon up to this houi
      For eight guilders, I never could learn,
      In faft it's a thing wherewith I've no concern.

CHAPTER XXIII.

How Hieronimus became domeſtic scribe to an old gentle-
man, who had a chambermaid, named **Amelia**; *and*
how he behaved himself well till the following chap-
ter.

A MONG all the ſundry and manifold ſtations
Of thoſe who dwell in theſe earthly habitations,
  Without any doubt we may ſafely call
  The widow's eſtate the ſaddeſt of all.

2. When the man, as the head of the woman, is taken
  Away, the whole body appears forſaken
    By its natural protector quite,
    And nothing in the houſe goes right.

3. The family is ſtraitened and haraſſed,
  The houſehold economy greatly embaraſſed,
    And all is care and ſorrow below
    And earth becomes a vale of woe.

4. Poor Mrs. **Jobs,** alas! was fated
  To experience the truth juſt ſtated,
    For all went crab-wiſe in the houſe
    And ſhe became as poor as a church mouſe.

9

5. Of courſe Hieronimus made his contribution
   To the general ſtock of deſtitution,
      For he lived as gentlemen of leiſure do,
      Ate well and drank ſtill better, too.

6. Meanwhile ſuch houſekeeping every hour
   To the worthy widow grew more and more ſour,
      And no one feature in it was wuſs
      Than the board of Hieronimus.

7. His own conviction grew daily ſtronger,
   That things could not go on ſo much longer,
      And he therefore began to look round
      To ſee if another opportunity could not be found.

8. As, now, in general, the rogues and the dunces
   Find in this world the very beſt chances,
      It happened that an opening offered again
      For Hieronimus with a nobleman.

9. This gentleman lived on his plantation
   In a quiet and retired ſituation,
      And there, as a genteel cavalier
      Spent his large income with *plaiſir*.

10. He is mentioned, in his youth, as engaging
    In the ſeven years' war which then was waging,
       But he ſtaid in garriſon moſtly, it is ſuppoſed,
       And his perſon was very little expoſed.

11. But he was very glad when the war was over,
    Being of peace an exceeding lover,
       In fact, as a brave man and wife one, too,
       He anticipated it, and withdrew.

12. And yet he loved to dwell on the ſtory
    Of the battles that had covered him with glory,
       And how when once he had bravely fought
       In the retreat he was almoſt caught.

13. For the reſt he was a man of ſportive habits,
    Shot occaſionally hares and rabbits,
       Drank at dinner Burgundy of his own,
       And lived without any wife alone.

14. He was, in ſo far, an old bachelor; however
    He had in the place of a wife a clever
       Chambermaid, who early and late
       On his urgent neceſſities did wait.

15. He had gradually as he felt himſelf growing older,
    Slipped all care of buſineſs off his ſhoulder,
       But he had of ſervant men a pair
       Who of all things took faithful care.

16. The one of them was a ſly old foxy,
    Steward of the houſe and general proxy,
       And the other Mr. Servant, he
       Was one they called a ſecretary.

17. The ſteward at the time of which we're ſpeaking,
    Still lived and found in his office good picking,
       For he took good care of cheſt and ſhelf,
       Thought leſs of his maſter and more of himſelf.

18. But the above mentioned ſecretary
    They had had, ſome days before, to bury,
       Becauſe he was dead, which cauſed there to be
       In this weighty office a vacancy.

19. Now the fteward aforefaid had long been acquainted
    With Hieronimus's parents, and therefore painted,
        As a true and accommodating man,
        Hieronimus in the beft colors he can.

20. And very earneftly recommended him,
    And fhortly in perfonâ prefented him
        To the damfel and the old gentleman, too,
        As the moft capable fecretary he knew.

21. The chambermaid found his perfon quite ftriking,
    And took to him confiderable liking,
        She therefore promifed, faithful and true,
        To fpeak the beft word for him that fhe knew.

22. The moment fhe faw him fhe liked him very
    Much better than the previous fecretary ;
        For Hieronimus was tall and ftrong,
        But his predeceffor was lean and long.

23. Since now, the old gentleman, as we made mention,
    Honored the damfel with his principal attention,
        He with favour her application heard,
        And gave Hieronimus a nobleman's word.

24. And further to fhow him the greater honour,
    He invited him the firft day to dinner,
        And then the old gent, when dinner was done,
        Said to him in a friendly tone :

25. His duty would confift in attending
    To the live ftock and feeing what wanted mending,
        And whatever was to be written, he
        Would write as private fecretary.

26. And if now this official duty
     Hieronimus did faithfully execute, he
         Would pay him, as a falary,
         Forty rix-dollars annually.

27. " If you like thefe conditions (faid he,) you can tarry
     With me *fub titulo* houfe-fecretary,
         And I alfo promife you, if true,
         Many additional perquifites, too ;

28. " But never go hazing, now **remember,**
     With the damfel that takes charge of the chamber
         For fuch proceedings will bring you into difgrace,
         I tell you dryly to your face.

29. "**The late, deceafed houfe-fecretary,**
     Was fond of damfels and young **women very,**
         And I was very much mortified to find
         That he to my maid was fecretly inclined.

30. " I fhould, therefore, at once have cafhiered him
     And without ceremony cleared him
         Out, but I faw he was weak and **flim,**
         And fo overlooked the fault in him.

31. " The girl, in truth, is fly and witty,
     But fomewhat deceitful, more's the pity,
         And indeed I have often fufpected that fhe
         Was given to all forts of monkery.

32. "**I** accidentally fell in with her
     Five years ago, as we journeyed together ;
         I was pleafed with the manner of the jade,
         And fo I took her for my maid.

33. "For the reſt, without a ſingle queſtion,
    You will hear now my concluding ſuggeſtion;
      For I tell you finally once for all,
      Have nothing to do with Amelia at all!"

34. Hieronimus muſt have been half-witted,
    Had he not on the conditions above ſubmitted,
      Accepted very willingly
      The part of private ſecretary.

35. He therefore entered on his office right gaily,
    And ſaw to the cows and the fences daily,
      And many notes he daily took
      And wrote in the memorandum book.

36. For example: packets that came by the ſtages,
    Money paid out for servants' wages,
      The hares that were ſhot and the turkey cocks,
      And when they picked the old gentleman's locks.

37. Or what the houſe advocate got for his pleadings,
    Or the judge obtained by extra proceedings,
      Or what amount at the market was paid
      For butter and cheeſe in lawful trade.

38. Or what Amelia's dreſſes coſt to cut 'em,
    Or lengthen 'em out at the top and bottom,
      Or widen 'em an inch and a-half,
      Or when the cow had had a calf.

39. Or when the worthy damſel had needed
    On account of fever to be bleeded,
      Or a hen had laid an egg; in ſhort,
      All incomes and outgoes of every ſort.

40. And where any letters needed inditing,
    The old gentleman, who was no hand at writing,
        Threw all upon Hieronimus,
        Who managed it all without any fufs.

41. With the help of **Talander he** wrote **them fafter**
    And quicker by far than any fchoolmafter,
        (**And** fpent lefs time about them **too**)
        Than any fchoolmafter **I** **ever knew.**

42. The reft of the time he fpent at his leifure,
    Ate and drank and flept at pleafure,
        So that he hoped he fhould **never give up,**
        As long as he lived, this fecretaryfhip.

Note.

Stanza 41. *Talander* **was** probably fome well-known author of a " Letter-writer." **The** original fimply mentions his *Brieffteller*.

CHAPTER XXIV.

How curious things befel the Secretary Hieronimus, and
he was driven away.

INDULGENT reader! our old forefathers
Were furely not dunces above all others,
   Far oftener will it rather be found
   That they had notions both wife and found.

2. And many a time we find them giving
   To us their pofterity rules of good living,
     And proverbs full of excellent ftuff,
     Which prove their wifdom plainly enough.

3. There is one old proverb much celebrated,
   And in all countries circulated,
     Of which the truth and certainty lies,
     Every day, before everybody's eyes.

4. Namely : "whoever can bear in fucceffion
   A long unbroken continuation
     Of nothing but profperous days, the fame
     Muft be gifted with a very ftrong frame."

5. The truth of this old proverb, thus early,
   Will in the prefent chapter clearly
     Make itfelf manifeft to us
     In the cafe of Hieronimus.

6. He lived like a prince, as much a ftranger
   To want, as a rat in a well filled manger,
      Went early to bed and flowly crept
      From the feathers on which he fo cofily flept.

7. There was nothing in fact to his comfort wanting;
   Only one thing his mind would be haunting,—
      The image of the damfel always was nigh,
      Whom he daily ogled with loving eye.

8. And in her looks and her whole expreffion
   He thought he was able to read a confeffion
      That fhe with him, the fecretary,
      Was in love, likewife, mortally.

9. And often, too, when he looked more nearly
   Into her face and ftudied it clearly,
      It always feemed to him more and more,
      As if he had feen her fomewhere before.

10. Defpite the old gentleman's prohibition,
    He ventured now on a declaration,
       And foon the knot of intimacy was tied
       As clofe as if they were bridegroom and bride.

11. But, in the old gentleman's prefence, he never
    Seemed to take any notice of her whatever;
       And very great care he always took
       Not to excite fufpicion even by a look.

12. Neverthelefs, when alone together
    They had many fly jokes with one another,
       And there paffed not feldom a friendly bufs
       'Twixt Amelia and Hieronimus.

13. That fhe meanwhile the old gentleman flattered
Before his face, it nothing mattered
　　To the fecretary, who held her free
　　For all this empty flattery.

14. In return for all his friendly attention
She gave him gifts too numerous to mention,
　　Shirts and handkerchiefs, gloves and rings,
　　Caps and cravats and all forts of things.

15. Once, on a time, when he had occafion
In his regular official vocation,
　　Some writing for her to defpatch,
　　She handed him a firft-rate watch.

16. He thanked her for it very fincerely,
But when in his hand he held it more nearly,
　　He cried: " *Potz taufend Element!* I'm fure,
　　I muft have feen this watch before!"

17. Amelia was ftartled beyond expreffion,
But made forthwith a candid confeffion,
　　That the watch in queftion, as a prefent, fhe
　　Had received from a ftudent formerly.

18. "How things do often happen queerly,
We fee in this inftance very clearly,"
　　Replied Hieronimus; "for certainly
　　That ftudent you before you fee."

19. And fo they both now calculated
That five years back their acquaintance dated,
　　And the watch that was ftolen fo long before
　　The damfel made a joke of,——— no more.

20. And both of them now made themſelves **merry,**
    And thought the joke was comical very,
        That, after travelling ſo far round,
        The watch ſhould in the right hands be found,

21. For the reſt there was nothing very ſurpriſing
    In the chambermaid's not recognizing
        In the ſecretary and candidate,
        The ſtudent ſhe met in that diſmal ſtate.

22. This laughable affair, however,
    Made them henceforth better friends than evei,
        And the flirtation they carried **on**
        Made **a** perfeſt fool of the old gentleman.

23. **Their** intercourſe, in **its familiarity,**
    Soon **took on** an air of bold hilarity,
        Till their courting and coquetting came to be
        Almoſt undiſguiſedly free.

24. If the damſel in cellar or **garden was** working,
    Mr. Secretary near ſomewhere was lurking,
        In kitchen and chamber and all about
        He ſtill tagged after her in-doors and out.

25. **And** even at night, when ſhe was not fuſſing
    About the old man, (for he needed much nurſing),
        Hieronimus ſometimes went
        On a viſit to her apartmént.

26. **Alſo,** in writing and noting, to guide him
    Amelia conſtantly ſat beſide him,
        In faſt, whether ſitting or ſtanding, ſhe
        Was at his ſide inceſſantly.

27. With many a tit-bit of dainty favour
    From the old man's table fhe did him favour,
        And was there calve's-head or the like of that,
        He always got the marrow and fat.

28. And fometimes fhe would bring him, on Sunday,
    Privately, from the cellar, a flafk of Burgundy,
        Which Hieronimus would drink
        At a couple of fwigs, and never wink.

29. Thus did the days of the houfe fecretary,
    Hieronimus, glide away, quite merry,
        No reverend prelate could poffibly
        Lead a more jolly life than he.

30. But it foon appeared that this fituation
    Of things could not be of long duration,
        For gradually the tranfaction began
        To grow more clear to the old gentleman.

31. And inftead of laughing, in fuch cafes,
    He now began to make four faces,
        And he gave them to underftand clearly enough,
        That he would not have any more of this ftuff.

32. And he added, in a manner not very
    Gentle, to Mr. Secretary,
        If he did not all intercourfe with Amelia quit,
        His walking-ticket he foon would get.

33. Hieronimus affured him on his honour,
    He had not behaved improperly in any manner,
        And he would not, if his Highnefs preferred,
        Exchange with Amelia another word.

34. "Well! in that cafe, you may tarry
 As long as you pleafe, and be fecretary
  All your life to me," replied
  The old gentleman, fomewhat mollified.

35. Although now, from this time Hieronimus
 Carried on his tricks as flyly **as any moufe,**
  With the damfel, by day and night,
  And did more diligently than ever write ;

36. Neverthelefs, not many days after,
 Occurred an adventure too ferious for laughter,
  When the old gentleman who, it feems,
  Was troubled with uncomfortable dreams,

37. Rofe and went up, as was his cuftom,
 To call Amelia who nurfed him,
  That the damfel by her friendlinefs
  Might drive away his fleepleffnefs,

38, Lo and behold ! a mighty wonder !
 For there, by fome unexpected blunder,
  Whom fhould he, to his amazement, fee,
  But Hieronimus, the fecretary !

39. *Himmel ! taufend Element ! potz donner !*
 The old gentleman fwore in fome fuch manner,
  And from the houfe, the felf fame night,
  Hieronimus was forced to take flight.

40. No begging nor praying the matter mended;
 The thing was done and there it ended,
  And the old man's wrath was fuch that the maid
  Began herfelf to be afraid.

41. Her cunning flatteries, however,
    Did once again for this time fave her,
       But the unlucky candidate
       Was paft all help, 'twas now too late.

NOTE.

Stanza 18.   The reader is requefted to obferve that in the firft line *how* qualifies *queerly*.

CHAPTER XXV.

*How Hieronimus entered into the service of a pious lady,
who was a spiritual sister, and had unworthy designs
upon him, and how he ran away from her.*

THE shirts, rings and other paraphernalia
Which Hieronimus had received from **Amelia**
    Served for some time to keep him free
    From the actual clutches of poverty.

2. But when, at last, he had sold and squandered
All the good damsel had to him tendered,
    Nolens volens, now must he,
    To escape from hunger and misery,

3. And not to die of absolute starvation,
Begin to look round for a new occupation,
    And his first thought, of course, was to try to find
    Some place of service to suit his mind.

4. Now, at a solitary castle there resided
A widowed lady who was a decided
    Spiritual sister, as we say,
    She was old and her hair already gray.

5. To praying and finging fhe therefore had taken
   And other things which as fpiritual we reckon,
      And fo a number of years had fpent
      And gained the name of a very great faint.

6. Not the leaft fhadow of fin could venture
   Among her little houfehold to enter,
      She called them together twice a day
      Into her parlor to fing and pray.

7. She punifhed them for the fmalleft violations
   Of duty by amiably ftinting their rations,
      She thought much of fafts and pfalmody
      And a glafs of brandy occafionally.

8. At the fame time, and with reafon, thinking
   That focial was better than folitary drinking,
      And alfo that in society
      One could fing with greater energy,

9. She had for fome time been defiring,
   And all the country round inquiring,
      To find fome holy man, that he
      Might give her his fpiritual company.

10. Already had many a godly loafer
    Prefented himfelf and made his offer,
       To live with her and praife and pray
       In the moft approved and orthodox way.

11. But no one as yet had had attraction
    Enough to give her fatisfaction,
       For this one feemed to her too old,
       The other by far too young, he was told;

12. One was too meagre, another too **weakly,**
One was a cripple or otherwife fickly,
Another was deaf or dumb or blind,
Another a **worlding, not at all to her mind.**

13. Hieronimus finally ventured therefore
His fervices to the dame to offer,
As fpiritual affiftant, and lo and **behold!**
So foon as fhe faw him, his fortune was told.

14. For he was neither meagre **nor weakly,**
Deaf nor dumb nor blind nor fickly,
Neither too **young** nor yet too old,
And his **perfon** was not uncomely to behold.

15. His **femi-clerical** peruke and garment
Took **the** old lady's eye in a moment,
And he affured her faithfully
That he was **no worlding,** no, not he.

16. And fo fhe gave him **an invitation**
To make to-day his **firft probation,**
And he joined with real, holy **glee**
The pious pfalmody **after tea.**

17. He alfo read with **edification**
A family **fermon to the** congregation,
And officiated **throughout** with fuch grace,
That **the dame** commended him to his face.

18. Her fpiritual zeal grew daily more fervent
Through the **labors** of this her godly fervant,
And every day a holier **flame**
Burned in her fpiritual frame.

19. She kept the pious young man befide her
    In all her actions to counfel and guide her,
       And thus Hieronimus foon became
       A very great favorite of the dame.

20. If, once in a while, fome deviation
    Occurred, unworthy of his vocation,
       She overlooked fuch things and would call
       Them human frailties—that was all.

21. She would alfo grant him difpenfations
    From the penalties fixed for fuch occafions,
       And at fuch times the daintieft fare
       By way of folace, fell to his fhare.

22. Champagne and chocolate and coffee,
    And almond milk and fuch rich ftuff, he
       Got for his beverage every day,
       And lived in an extra-luxurious way.

23. He found, in a word, a high enjoyment
    In purfuing fuch a holy employment,—
       Eating and drinking all day long,
       With, occafionally, a fermon or fong.

24. The worft thing was that the pious matron
    Kept him tied to the ftrings of her apron,
       For fhe really feemed to think that he
       Was the beau ideal of piety.

25. And when on the fofa he fate befide her,
    And read fome book that edified her,
       She would ftroke her pious fheep and fay:
       Bravo! in a very rapturous way.

26. And when they fang a holy meafure
    Together, fhe could not **contain** her pleafure,
      She would throw her arm around his neck,
      And fing, as if her heart would break.

27. This **very** familiar ftyle of aftion,
    At laft revealed the whole tranfaftion
      To Hieronimus, that the old dame
      At fomething **more than finging did aim.**

28. With fuch a weighty difcovery **before** him,
    A violent fit of **alarm came** o'er **him,**
      And **when** on **the mighty danger he** thought
    He was almoft paralyfed on the fpot.

29. When once recovered from his confternation,
    He thought, with many **a tender** fenfation,
      Of the blifs he had tafted formerly
      In the fair Amelia's company.

30. She was young and faultlefs and charming,
    This one, on the contrary, almoft alarming,
      Gray and toothlefs and yellow of fkin,
      Lean and haggard and ugly as fin.

31. He fhould, perhaps, have tutored his fancies
    And, adapted himfelf to circumftances,
      And, blinking at all her foibles and flaws,
    Taken the old lady as fhe was;

32. But this did not fuit his difpofition,
    So he came away without afking difmiffion,
      And left the old lady alone, alas!
      With her hymn-book and her brandy-glafs.

CHAPTER XXVI.

How Hieronimus had a bad and a good adventure, and how, for once in his life, he achieved a wife action.

HIERONIMUS, before he decided
  To leave the old widow, had provided
    A bag of money, deducting the fame
    From the private treafury of the dame.

2. For he argued that all his finging and praying,
    And holy things in fermons faying,
      And receiving the old lady's careffes, too,
      Made a fair compenfation no more than his due.

3. And now with the fruits of this handfome pillage
    He travelled about from city to village,
      And as in this way he wandered round
      Full many a jolly landlord he found.

4. And when he found in one place or another
    Fine quarters and fometimes a merry brother,
      Or a hoftefs agreeable in her ways,
      He commonly tarried feveral days.

5. It happened, however, on one occafion,
    That as he thus wandered for recreation,
      Juft as the fhades of evening fell
      He ftopped at quite a large hotel.

6. It was the beſt tavern in all Swabia,
   No better could be found in the wilds of Arabia;
      The hoſt was an honeſt man in his talk
      And loved to write with double chalk.

7. Now that ſame day, it did befal ſo,
   That two ſtrange gueſts had arrived there alſo,
      Who, Hieronimus did gueſs,
      Were travelling merchants, by their dreſs.

8. In one of them, at the very firſt entrance,
   He would almoſt have ſeen an old acquaintance,
      Had not a great plaſter on the place,
      Disguiſed about one-half of his face.

9. Meanwhile the two gentlemen grew quite merry,
   And invited Hieronimus to partake of their ſherry,
      And very ſoon a friendſhip grew
      Between Hieronimus and the two.

10. For the man who had on his face the plaſter,
    Was, in telling ſtories, a very great maſter,
       Some he made up and others were true;
       Hieronimus laughed till he was almoſt blue.

11. Hieronimus, in his turn, freely related
    All his adventures and communicated
       How very near he recently came
       To being decoyed by a widowed dame.

12. There followed, of courſe, a peal of laughter,
    And Hieronimus, thereafter,
       Proceeded to make the ſtory whole
       By telling about the money he ſtole.

13. Now when the day, in a manner ſo cheery,
    Had come to a cloſe, Hieronimus, weary
        And drunk with wine and laughter, ſaid
        Good night and ſtaggered off to bed.

14. But hardly had he ſunk to ſlumber,
    When the two gentlemen proceeded to his chamber,
        Where they ingeniouſly did hook
        The money, and their departure took.

15. Hieronimus, waking late in the morning,
    And having of mischief not the leaſt warning,
        Found, as he put his pantaloons on
        His pocket empty, the money-bag gone.

16. At firſt he could not believe the tranſaction
    A real caſe for a legal action,
        He thought it only a piece of fun
        Which the two merry merchants had done.

17. But when the hoſt, interrogated
    Reſpecting them, communicated
        That the two gentlemen went away
        Quickly at an early hour of the day ;—

18. Then did he begin to make lamentations
    And outcries great, and his impatience
        Grew to ſuch a pitch that the hair
        On his head could be kept with difficulty there.

19. His crying and groaning in ſuch a faſhion,
    Soon ſtirred the worthy hoſt to compaſſion,
        Who agreed to take only his coat in lieu
        Of the money that for board was due.

20. And alfo the advice imparted
    That it were well now, if he ftarted,
       "For without the ready cafh," faid **he,**
       "**No ftranger can find quarters with me.**"

21. Hieronimus's example teaches how odd is,
    In this world, the caprice of the bandaged goddess,
       And how, in a manner unlooked for and ftrange,
       The luck of mortals will often change.

22. Laft evening the thought of poverty fcorning,
    Called "Sir" by the landlord, and lo! **this morning,**
       By the fame worthy landlord hurled
       Coatlefs and pennilefs out into the world.

23. He could now, as he refumed his wandering,
    On his fad eftate at leifure be pondering,
       And at firft he almoft wifhed **himfelf back**
       (At the fpiritual fifter's, alack!)

24. But when he thought of her careffes,
    And called up her image in memory's receffes,
       Such a real horror came over him **then,**
       That he did not care to go back again.

25. He had now, for fome days, contrived to banifh
    His hunger with an acorn or turnip or radifh,
       And like a knight errant had managed to ftay
       His nature in many a pitiful way.

26. But now, as when the need is higheft,
    The confolation is apt to be nigheft,
       So was it in poor Hieronimus's cafe
       The help he required was coming apace.

27. For as, on the fourth afternoon, he was lying
    In a wood by the roadſide, he heard a crying
       Very loud and piteous indeed,
       Which from near by did ſeem to proceed.

28. He ſoon arrived at the ſituation
    Whence he had heard the lamentation,
       And there, to his very great ſurpriſe,
       A harrowing ſpectacle met his eyes:

29. A carriage with four horſes ſtopping;
    A bearded coachman powerleſs dropping;
       There a young lady, who ſhrieked and cried,
       And ran deſpairing from ſide to ſide.

30. And here a richly dreſſed gentleman, ſtriving
    To keep off two ruffians who at him were driving,
       And who were ſeeking with might and main,
       To give him his *quietus*, 'twas plain.

31. My hero recognized at ſome diſtance,
    The *quaſi* merchants, his tavern acquaintance,
       He therefore lifted his ſtick, and flew
       At once, like a fury, upon the two.

32. "Villains! where is my bag of money?"
    He cried, and darting upon one, he
       Shattered his ſkull ſo that it couldn't be trepanned
       And ſtretched the robber dead on the ſand.

33. With equally vigorous blows he darted
    At t'other robber, who ſtraightway ſtarted,
       Finding himself outmatched in fight,
       And proceeded to ſeek his ſafety in flight.

34. Hieronimus would, without hefitating,
    Have chafed the highwayman who was retreating,
    But the fellow vanifhed like **the wind,**
    And left Hieronimus far behind.

35. **And now I** can fcarcely defcribe the behaviour
    Of the gentleman and lady to their faviour,
    When, the imminent peril being o'er,
    They felt that they could breathe once **more.**

36. They **thanked him,** both of them, very fincerely,
    And the pretty girl would have kifsed him nearly,
    If (to fay the truth) fhe had not feared
    His unwafhed face and his grifly **beard.**

37. No eulogy can be invented
    Which was not by them to him prefented,
    For the dear Hieronimus, dirty and rough
    Was their deliverer, clearly enough.

38. He muft go home with them, they infifted,
    With a friendlinefs that could not be refifted,
    To their manor-houfe, where he fhould be
    Richly rewarded for his chivalry.

39. In his prefent impoverifhed **circumftances**
    He received with open arms thefe advances,
    And, without further ceremony, thought beft
    At once to comply with their requeft.

40. Lifting the coachman they conveyed him
    To the carriage in which they laid him,
    And, donning the dead highwayman's coat,
    Up on the box Hieronimus got.

41. Before, however, Hieronimus mounted,
    He found, with a pleafure not to be recounted,
    His bag and almoft all the money, too,
    In the dead highwayman's portmanteau.

42. But the ftrangeft thing in all the hiftory
    Was, touching the dead man's face, a myftery;
    There was no longer any plafter there,
    And when Hieronimus scanned it with care,

43. He was not long in taking knowledge
    Of a gentleman who, on his journey to college,
    Once fwindled him by hook and by crook,
    Herr von Hogier of the great peruke.

44. And fo this adventure terminated
    In a way that our hero greatly elated,
    He mounted the coach-box and off he rolled,
    Like the knight of the forrowful figure of old.

45. And now ere I bring this chapter to a termination,
    I inform the readers of the prefent narration,
    That this deed is the only honorable one
    That Hieronimus has hitherto done.

CHAPTER XXVII.

How Hieronimus was glad to get to Ohnewitz, and how
he became schoolmaster there, in a school of little boys
and girls.

T HAT gentleman and the young lady
 Whom Hieronimus refcued, as mentioned already,
  Suftained the relation of bridegroom and bride
  And the knot had been very recently tied.

2. The gentleman had in his jurisdiction
   Of caſtles and villages quite a collection,
      But the principal one of his private ſeats
      Was in the ſmall village of Ohnewitz.

3. To give his lady a gratification
   He often made journeys of recreation,
      For on very intimate terms he ſtood
      With every body in his neighborhood.

4. He had juſt been to viſit a neighboring noble
   At the time he met the aforeſaid trouble,
      'Twas on his journey home from the ſame,
      That the two highwaymen upon him came.

5. They immediately knocked the driver over,
   So that they thought he would never recover;
      And with violence then demanded next,
      His money and other perſonal effects.

6. They alſo from the carriage hauled him,
   And would to death have probably mauled him,
      When, at the ſhrieks of the agonized dame,
      Hieronimus, as we ſaid, to the reſcue came.

7. They related, on the way, this ſtory
   To their deliverer, who in his glory
      Drove away as merrily now
      As the recent terror would allow.

8. Hieronimus likewiſe recounted
   How he by the fates had been thus far tormented,
      And as, in this way time, quickly flits,
      They came, like lightning, to Ohnewitz.

9. Here they foon forgot all forrow,
   And lived without a thought of the morrow,
      And made all forts of friendly fufs
      In honor to Hieronimus.

10. New clothes, wine, tobacco and coftly difhes,
    Calculated to gratify the moft faftidious wifhes,
       Were furnifhed, enough and fuperfluous,
       At the fervice of Hieronimus.

11. After feveral weeks had been fpent in this manner,
    The gentleman did Hieronimus the honour,
       To promife that he, for his future **fupport,**
       Would make provifion in the very beft fort.

12. Now juft at this time an event tranfpired,
    Juft what Hieronimus would have defired,
       And he faw in the coincidence
       The hand of a fpecial Providence.

13. Namely : the Ohnewitz parifh pofsefses
    A fchool for little mafters and mifses,
       Of which the collation unto the **lord,**
       As village patron, the laws did **accord.**

14. To ftudy the A, B, C, and the primer,
    And learn to read and fpell, and the grammar,
       Thefe branches conftituted the whole
       Of the ftudies purfued at the aforefaid fchool.

15. All opportunities of further learning
    The patron removed, with a wife difcerning,
       For whenever a peafant comes to be learned,
       At once he grows proud and his brain is turned.

16. Yes, experience teaches us plainly,
    That what the peafant requires mainly
        Is to underftand his almanack, and
        To have his catechifm at his tongue's end.

17. Whenever above this limit he rifes,
    His labour he commonly defpifes,
        And a miferable confufion enfues
        With the farming proceeds and revenues.

18. Befides a fixum of thirty dollars, the office
    Brought the teacher additional profits
        In eggs and butter and turkeys and geefe
        And other perquifites fimilar to thefe.

19. And then, at the new year's congratulation,
    He went to his lordfhip's houfe to collation,
        And alfo received, for attending there,
        Of prefents a proportionate fhare.

20. Now the fchoolmafter happened, fortunately,
    To have left this world his blefling lately,
        And the parifh was thoughtfully looking round
        To fee where a new one might be found.

21. So foon as the patron got information
    Of this, he tendered the fituation
        To Hieronimus, who ftraightway
        Entered on the office without delay.

22. At firft, it is true, the life of a teacher
    Had not for him one attractive feature,
        For he much more account of idlenefs made
        Than of fuch a thanklefs and tedious trade.

23. However, as always, when fchool was over,
    He spent his time at the castle in clover,
    Eating and drinking, after awhile
    Hieronimus concluded to reconcile

24. Himself to his prefent fituation,
    And attend to its duties with renewed application,
    That he might be able to keep the place
    All his life till the end of his days.

25. He alfo thought, in many a matter,
    To introduce fome change for the better;
    For he found that many faults had crept
    Into the fchool, as heretofore kept.

26. In fact he began, after long deliberation,
    To make here and there a reformation,
    Which did not, however, turn out very well,
    As we to the reader fhall fhortly tell.

NOTE.

Heading: *Ohnewitz* means literally *witlefs.*

CHAPTER XXVIII.

*How Hieronimus became an Author, and how he edited
a new A, B, C,-book, and how he was grievoufly
complained of for it by the Boors to his Lordfhip.*

A T the very firſt entrance on his adminiſtration
Hieronimus found with extremeſt vexation,
    That the A, B, C-book hitherto uſed
    The minds of the children ſomewhat confuſed

2. The boys and girls under his ſupervisſion
   Had uſed heretofore the Ballhorn edition,
      In which Hieronimus ſoon became aware
      Of sundry errors here and there.

3. So, after conſiderable counſel taking
   With himſelf, he determined upon making
      A ſpeedy new edition of it
      Under the following title, to wit :

4. *A new, enlarged and amended edition*
   Of the A, B, C-book, under the ſupervisſion
      Of the Author, Hieronimus
      Jobs, Theologiæ Candidatus.

5. To the letters with which we're all acquainted,
   And which in the alphabet are preſented,
      He added alſo the f f t,
      Likewiſe the ſch and ſp.

6. The ſpurs of the cock, at the end, who engages
   The attention of children of the lower ages,
      He omitted with great propriety
      From his bran-new book of A, B, C

7. He added, however, for the gratification
   Of the juvenile candidates for education,
      A little neſt with a great egg,
      Beſide the ſpurleſs rooſter's leg.

8. This book had ſcarcely entered their presence,
   When it was reviewed by the Ohnewitz peaſants,
      And the very firſt occaſion gave
      For an altercation both fierce and grave.

9. For none of the changes made, whatever,
   Found with the critics any favour,
      But they every one of them, to a man,
      Regarded it as a highly dangerous plan.

10. It could not efcape the obtufeft vifion,
    That the author of this new-fangled edition,
       Made it exceedingly manifeft,
       He was with a paffion for authorfhip poffeffed.

11. As, when, in fultry fummer weather,
    Tempeft-brewing vapors mufter together,
       Before the crafhing thunder leaps,
       A low murmur ordinarily creeps,

12. So here, at firft, in every direction
    Was heard a low buzz of difaffection,
       And foon the thunderbolt came down
       On Hieronimus's crown.

13. The Ohnewitzers by words and dealings
    Left him no doubt of the ftate of their feelings,
       But he, defying their utmoft rage,
       Fell back on his Grace's patronage.

14. The Ohnewitzers would fhow him, however,
    That they did not mean to be filent forever:
       For every day they did prefer
       Some new grievance againft the fchoolmaftér.

15. They therefore, at laft, in town meeting collected,
    And the fexton was unanimoufly directed
       To draw up a complaint in the following tone:
       " High-well-born patron! be it known

16. " *Unto your worſhip by theſe* **preſents,—**
    That we the aſſembled Ohnewitz peaſants
      Do take with ſubmiſſion the liberty
      To complain of your ſchoolmaſter to thee.

17. " Inasmuch as the fame has tried our patience
    By introducing ſundry innovations,
      All under the abſurd pretext
      Of remedying exiſting **defeēts.**

18. " And has not behaved in the matter, neither,
    As a worthy ſchoolmaſter ſhould, but rather,
      Given us peaſants, whom he ought to lead,
      A very bad example indeed.

19. " And, only the principal points to mention
    Of the grievances to which we would call attention,
      Pro primo and in the firſt place, he
      Has undertaken arbitrarily

20. " To make a new A, **B, C,** omitting
    The ſpurs of the cock, which is not befitting,
      For the ſpurs, aſſuredly, all will agree
      An eſſential part of the cock to be.

21. " He alſo diſcourages learning, however,
    By making the alphabet longer then ever:
      For ſp, ſch, and ſft
      Have ſurely no buſineſs in the A, B, C.

22. " Further, though cocks are never known to
    Lay hen's eggs in neſts, as hens are wont to,
      Neverthelefs he has placed one by the cock's leg,
      Juſt as if the cock had laid the egg.

23. "Now things like thefe are very bewilderin',
    And calculated to miflead the minds of the children,
    And a new A, B, C-book, anyhow,
    Is an innovation we cannot allow.

24. "*Pro fecundo:* we would not fail to mention
    (That the afs's head is an ancient invention,)
    Which every child that refifts the rules
    Has to wear, as a punifhment, in our fchools.

25. "Now, forely as a fenfitive heart is affected
    When to this punifhment it is fubjected,
    Still moft of the children make a jeft
    Of wearing the afs's head down to their breaft.

26. "Herr Jobs, however, is not contented
    With this, but has to the head appended
    Neck, body, legs and tail and all
    And fo you have now the afs in full.

27. "How the children cry and yell when the teacher
    Compels them to wear the entire creature,
    And the figure they cut when dreffed up fo,
    Can be fcarcely imagined. *Pro tertio:*

28. "Herr Jobs, in addition to the ufual feruling,
    Doth barbaroufly box their ears, imperilling
    The health of the pupils, and already fome
    In confequence have quite deaf become.

29. "*Pro quarto:* the poorer children more than any
    Are to be pitied for their cudgellings many,
    For, out of respect to perfons, they
    Get a double portion every day.

30. " *Pro quinto :* he is in the habit of fearchin'
    The pockets of every fweet-toothed urchin,
      And puts the apples and nuts on the fhelf,
      And after fchool he eats them himfelf.

31. " *Pro sexto :* his conduct in general fociety
    Is chargeable with much impropriety,
      For he leads, they fay, quite too free a life
      With Schulze the boarding-houfe keeper's wife.

32. " He vifits the village tavern daily
    And in heated drinks indulges freely,
      And many a time has wafted away
      Half of the night with Schulze in play.

33. " There are many other complaints, in addition,
    Which we would prefer with profound fubmiffion ;
      For very many *gravamina,*
      Befides thofe already mentioned, there are,

34. " Which at present, however, we forbear ftating,
    Contenting ourfelves with fupplicating :
      That you would be pleafed, moft gracious Sir !
      To give us another fchoolmaftér.

35. " In hope whereof we beg to tarry
    Your Grace's fubjects moft exemplary.
      Given in the village of Ohnewitz.
      Etc., etc., etc., etc., etc., etc., etc."

12

CHAPTER XXIX.

*How the difaffected peafants of Ohnewitz received a
gracious refolution, and how they were advifed to keep
filence, and how they were threatened with the dark
hole.   All in chancery ſtyle.*

THE meeting appointed a deputation
Of two to deliver the petition
   To his highnefs, the patron; and from the fame
   The following refolution came:

2. " *We have learned with great diſſatisfaĉtion,*
From the ftatement of your recent aĉtion,
   What grievances you do prefer
   Againft your worthy fchoolmafter.

ε. " Though, now, it gives us great difpleafure
To fee you refort to fuch a meafure;
   We have confidered, neverthelefs,
   The breadth and length of your grievances.

4. " We cannot, however, up to date difcover
Anything to make fuch a fufs over,
   And the profecution, we decide,
   Is altogether unjuftified.

5. " 'Tis very true, as has been faid, he
   Has introduced in his fchool already
     A new book of A, B, C, which he
     Dedicates to ourfelves fubmiffively.

6. " It is alfo clear that, in this edition,
   He has made here and there an addition or omiffion,
     It is not however fo clear to us,
     How this can be fo injurious.

7. " 'Tis true, by an overfight of the engraver,
   The cock has loft his fpurs; however,
     One can very eafily in the next
     Edition remedy fuch miftakes.

8. " Our modern reviewers feldom take notice
   Of fuch a trifle in books as that is,
     But the gentlemen kindly overlook
     Such little faults in a new book.

9. " And as regards the interpolations,
   They are found in all the early editions;
     At leaft fch, fft, and fp,
     As variations, may be fuffered to be.

10. " That the cock with an egg fhould be attended,
    Seems indeed lefs capable of being defended,
      Yet there's no neceffity *propter hoc*
      To take the egg away from the cock.

11. " For from the egg to draw the conclufion
    That the cock had laid it, were great confufion
      In confcience and reafon; it proves in fact
      No more than the titles to men's names tacked.

12. " And then befides we might have alluded,
    To cafes where cockerels over eggs have brooded,
    In hoc cafu, undoubtedly,
    The cock was a capon properly.

13. " When you propofe as the fecond of the abufes,
    That Mr. Jobs a whole afs introduces;
    We think therein he commits no offence,
    But conducts himfelf as a man of fenfe.

14. " For he means by this no more, nor lefs neither,
    Than that you and your children both together,
    Old and young and great and fmall,
    Are perfect affes incarnate all.

15. " *Pro tertio :* the ear-boxing fo bewilderin',
    Which has already made deaf fome children—
    We hold it very much amifs
    To inflict fuch punifhment as this.

16. " The grievance you have *pro quarto* propounded
    We hold to be in fo far well grounded ;
    For no judge nor fchoolmafter rightfully can
    Refpect the perfon of any man.

17. " But for poor no lefs than rich 'tis expedient
    That they fhould be punifhed when difobedient,
    And punifhment fhould always be
    Adminiftered impartially.

18. " When the right of fearch he exercifes,
    And fruit in the children's pockets furprifes,
    He upholds *pro quinto* the very good rule :
    Children fhould not be munching in school !

19. " And as their tender ſtomachs, ſans queſtion,
    Find apples and nuts of hard digeſtion,
      Here alſo the ſchoolmaſter's plan is good,
      To devour, himſelf, ſuch forbidden food.

20. " *Pro sexto*, as to your inſinuation
    Touching Schulze's wife's reputation,
      Item, the tavern, drinking and dice,
      All this in Herr Jobs were a ſhocking vice.

21. "It is our gracious pleaſure, however,
    That ſuch things be buried in ſilence forever,
      And whoſo ſhall name them again, by my ſoul!
      Shall be puniſhed with two days in the hole.

22. " For the reſt, the complaints you have delated
    Shall be hereafter more thoroughly inveſtigated,
      When from our contemplated tour
      We are happily returned once more.

23. " Till then we command you to ceaſe your gabble,
    Nor longer in theſe grave matters dabble.
      Given at our reſidence etc., ***etc.***"
    " Reſolution for the Peaſants of Ohnewitz."

CHAPTER XXX.

How, one Wednesday, a riot broke out at Ohnewitz, and
all sorts of signs and wonders preceded it, and how
Herr Hieronimus was driven away with cudgels, &c.

IT may well be conceived that this resolution
Threw the whole village into the greatest confusion,
   In fact there arose on all sides a hum
   Among the peasants, both mighty and grum.

2. For now it was clearly manifested
   That Jobs was by the patron assisted,
      And that justice could no longer have course,
      And they swore to avenge themselves by force.

3. In this weighty crisis they often came together
   To consult in the tavern with one another,
      And with beer and tobacco considered there
      How they could best approach the affair.

4. They first determined, with a sweeping
   Unanimity, on keeping
      Their children at home, and not one of all
      In fact went to school again, great or small.

5. But the wifeſt of them adviſed, with reaſon,
   To lie in wait for a favorable ſeaſon,
     For then, when came the fitting hour,
     They could all ariſe at once in their **power.**

6. They all gave in at once their adheſion
   To ſuch a ſenſible propoſition,
     And ſo they fixed upon a day
     When the patron ſhould happen to be away.

7. 'Tis true theſe arrangements were all to lie ſleeping,
   In every boſom's ſecret keeping
     Till the **terrible moon** ſhould be uſhered in
     When the diſturbance was to begin.

8. But before theſe great events had being,
   Signs and wonders had men been ſeeing,
     As on the eve of important events
     Men commonly witneſs premonitory porténts.

9. For example, a ſhort time before, at the hour
   Of midnight, a very great owl on the tower
     Of the church had been heard to utter a cry
     Frightful and loud to the inky ſky.

10. Likewiſe had one of the Ohnewitz people
    Coming from the inn, heard a tolling in the ſteeple;
      Alſo the very old chimney fell **down**
      On the ſchool-houſe roof with an awful ſound.

11. Likewiſe the ſexton's cow give birth to
    The longeſt **eared calf** perhaps on earth too;
      Likewiſe many dogs ran howling round
      Through the village **with a** horrible ſound.

12. Ignes fatui were feen in many places,
    And fometimes by night ftrange forms and faces ;
      Likewife at noonday it came to pafs,
      A leg was broke of the miller's afs.

13. All this appeared the prefiguration
    Of fome impending revelation ;
      But no one noticed the danger until
      The prophecies did themfelves fulfil.

14. Now it was exactly on Wednefday morning,
    That the riot broke out without any warning,
      When, at eight precifely, every boor
      Was feen to iffue from his door.

15. It was dreadful to think on what might happen,
    For every one was armed with a weapon,
      And forth the confederates all fwarmed,
      With clubs and flails in great numbers armed.

16. All was now aftir in the village,
    One would have prophefied murder **and** pillage,
      And every dog and roofter now
      Began at once to bark and crow.

17. On the village common foon collected
    The mighty mafs of the difaffected,
      And in proceffion proceeded thence
      Straight to the fchoolmafter's refidence.

18. Many children came thronging after
    On both fides, full of joy and laughter,
      To think that they would be free to-day
      And the bad fchoolmafter fent away.

19. Herr Jobs in his bed was lying quiet,
    Never once dreaming of any riot,
      When all on a fudden the whole fwarm
      Broke in upon him with a great alarm.

20. He opened his eyes in confternation,
    And vehement was his agitation,
      As now for the firft time he did mark
      The treafon that had been brewing in the dark.

21. They fell upon him with precipitation,
    Leaving him fmall time for hefitation;
      Only, in confideration of the prefent diftrefs,
      They gave him leave to put on his drefs:

22. Then advifed him to leave Ohnewitz behind him,
    And never again let one of them find him;
        They added likewife many a fcoff,
        And cudgelled and pelted our hero off.

23. And fo this action was completed
    And the expedition fuccefsfully treated,
        And with a loud ju! hu! ju! hu!
        All to the tavern now withdrew.

24. And every one fwore with a terrible clatter,
    That he had done the beft in the matter,
        And in drinking brandy determined that he
        The greateft hero of all would be.

25. There were fome, however, had no fatisfaction,
    But only remorfe for the whole tranfaction,
        And they fully expected to find their reward
        In the dark hole, at the return of their lord.

NOTE.

Stanza 9. So in Virgil (Aen. IV. 462,) among the por-
tents that preceded the death of Dido:

" *Solaque culminibus ferali carmine bubo*
Sæpe queri, et longas in fletum ducere voces."

                    —" With a boding note   .
The folitary fcreech-owl ftrains her throat,
And on a chimney's top or turret's height,
With fongs obfcene difturbs the filence of the night."—

                                        Dryden.

CHAPTER XXXI.

How Hieronimus in his flight to Bavaria and a new
adventure, in meeting his beloved Amelia on the stage
at the theatre. Very pleasant to read.

A S the fox, when he leaves the hounds behind him
And flies where they no more can find him,
  Is glad that only a mouthful of hair
  He has had to lose, which he well could spare,—

2. So Hieronimus, in his greatest tribulation,
Took to himself the same consolation,
  And was very glad, upon his soul,
  To have 'scaped the boors with a skin whole.

3. 'Tis true he had learned, in his sudden departure
From Ohnewitz, something he had to smart for,
  How very sour and bitter and hard
  Was a poor schoolmaster's reward.

4. He also made a vow that he never
Would publish again any books whatever,
  For his flogging and flight, he had to own,
  Were owing to the authorship-mania alone.

5. Meanwhile as his patron (we've ſtated already,)
  Was gone on a tour to Bavaria with his lady ;
    Hieronimus determined to go there to him,
    For refuge from the wrath of the peaſants ſo grim.

6. The journey took no great time to plan it,
  In fa&t he no ſooner reſolved than began it ;
    But ſoon, before he was far on his way,
    A new adventure cauſed his delay.

7. For contrary to all expe&tation
  His plans met a ſudden pertubation,
    Soon after he reached a great city, where
    He intended to reſt a day or two there.

8. Here, to conſole and divert himſelf ſolely
  And drive away care and melancholy,
    It came into his head one day,
    That he that evening would go to the play.

9. He ſoon perceived among the a&treſſes,
  Of beautiful faces and ſplendid dreſſes,
    One who in face, voice, form and hair,
    Was the image of his Amelia fair.

10. Heavens ! what rapture his heart did fire,
  That he ſhould ſo unexpectedly ſpy her !
    The entire pit was almoſt thrown
    Into confuſion by this fa&t alone.

11. And hardly had ſhe her performance ended,
  When into the green-room he inſtantly bounded,
    And now there was many a joyful buſs
    'Twixt her and her dear Hieronimus.

12. Both were curious to hear from each other,
   What fingular fortune thus brought them together;
      Hieronimus therefore was glad enough,
      With her to fnug quarters to hurry off.

13. Then and there did Amelia get her firft information
   Of the **wonders fet down** in the previous narration,
      As having tranfpired fince the memorable night,
      When the old gent drove him forth in fuch plight.

14. And of his adventures with the fpiritual lady,
   And the difhonorable attempt fhe made, he
      Told, and how, fubfequently, the whole
      Of his money by night in a tavern was ftole.

15. And how, in the wood he defpatched a villain,
   And refcued a nobleman whom he was killin',
      And became by one of his lucky hits,
      A fchoolmafter at Ohnewitz.

16. And his fubfequent trials and tribulation,
   And how he now againft all expeftation,
      Had found her in the theatre here,
      All this he copioufly poured in her ear.

17. Hieronimus, now, in his turn, defired
   To hear what in her experience had tranfpired,
      And the fair one proceeded to relate,
      As follows, her hiftory up to date.

CHAPTER XXXII.

How the damsel Amelia tells Hieronimus the story of her
life. A very long chapter, because the person speaking
is a female. Exactly one hundred verses.

" **A** MELIA Ripraps my proper name is :
    The place where into the world I came, is
    The celebrated town of A. A.
    There I firſt faw the light of day.

2. " My father was an advocate, had many cafes
   Both there and in the neighboring places,
   For he knew the *jura* thoroughly
   And underſtood chicanery.

3. " The moſt complicated cafes he would take'em
   And ſtill more complicated make'em,
   And many an art and trick he knew
   For ſpinning out ſhort cafes, too.

4. " His ingenuity many a clever
   Rogue from the gallows did deliver;
   And, by recommending the crime
   Of perjury juſt in the nick of time,

5. " He brought off many a cheat inglorious,
   Over his honorable opponent victorious,
   Relieved many a one of ſore diſtreſs
   And many a poor devil of his bread, I gueſs.

6. " He hated peace and compromiſing,
   Much rather, in every cafe, adviſing,
   However trifling the matter might be,
   Recourse to law and chicanery.

7. " He kept his clients in a round of dances
   Through all poſſible legal *inſtánces*,
   And kept them appealing, on and on,
   Until their very laſt penny was gone.

8. " For the reſt, he ſerved to the beſt of his ſcience
   And fidelity the clients who placed on him reliance,
   Yet, now and then, for variety's ſake,
   From the oppoſite party a bribe would take.

9. "Of a tolerable property he thus got poffeffion ;
   What to others was a curfe, was to him a bleffing,
   And when to wrangling and quarrelling fell,
   He took the oyfter and gave each a fhell.

10. "My bleffed mother was the daughter
    Of a wealthy farmer of the higheft order,
    Who litigated to fuch a degree
    That he ruined himfelf and his property.

11. "My father had ferved him as advocate duly
    And given him counfel faithfully and truly,
    And fo at length, he got for his pay
    The farmer's pretty daughter one day.

12. "She had already rejected many
    Who offered their hands in matrimony,
    At the time when her father was yet well off
    And had property enough.

13. "But as the incomes began to grow fewer,
    No one cared any longer to woo her ;
    For the prettieft pennilefs face that goes
    Will never tempt the men to propofe.

14. "She managed after awhile, however,
    To catch my father, for fhe was clever,
    And grounded to the laft degree
    In all the arts of gallantry.

15. "My father took a fancy to her,
    And fo, as aforefaid, became her wooer,
    And, wifhing a partner of his life,
    Befought her of the farmer for wife.

16. " They tafted together many enjoyments
In their wedded life, and little annoyance,
At leaft for the firft three months or fo,
While marriage was yet a new thing, you know.

17. " And then her fine face and agreeable manner
Many a private income won her,
When fome rich party happened to be
Attentive to her particularly.

18. They managed to get from parties in cafes
A matter or two for houfehold ufes;
For the advocate's lady always got
What the advocate, her Lord, did not.

19. " When her hufband to his pleadings attended,
She meanwhile was not idle-handed,
And at fuch times in her apartments fhe
Had private hearings generally.

20. " Now though I cannot pofitively declare it
For a faƌt, and folemnly fwear it,
That the above named advocate
Was my real father—at any rate

21. " I never in my life have heard the fuggeftion
That he fo much as raifed a queftion,
When, after about a year, may be,
My mother was delivered of me.

22. " The earlier parts of my childifh hiftory
Remain involved in the fhades of myftery,
However my father and mother loved me
As their only daughter tenderly.

13*

23. "No pains were fpared on the formation
    Of my manners and my education,
    And they fent me to fchool at an early age
    In the ufual ftudies there to engage.

24. "They ftrictly forbade, however, the teachers
    To inflict on me blows or bitter fpeeches,
    And in everything, fmall as it might be,
    My will was confulted carefully.

25. "When I fcarcely was ten years old, my fancies
    Began to devour all forts of romances,
    And already far more of love I knew
    Than other maidens of eighteen do.

26. "I was happy and vain to receive addreffes
    From pretty young men, and fometimes careffes,
    And many a practical romance
    In my thirteenth year did already commence.

27. "Perhaps 'twas a fault of my education,
    That I felt very early an inclination,
    Which never has yet my nature left,—
    A fecret inclination to theft.

28. "My parents, fmitten with fatal blindnefs,
    Called it childifh fport in their mifplaced kindnefs,
    And when I was caught in fome wicked craft,
    At their fly little daughter they only laughed.

29. "My fifteenth year was hardly over,
    When I had already many a lover,
    Which, with one of my not ugly face,
    Could hardly fail of being the cafe.

30. "Some of them feemed quite prefentable
 In my father's eyes, at leaft not contemptible;
   My mother, however, found in the fame
   Many a thing to diflike and blame.

31. "It muft be a man of high pofition,
 Equal to any in the land in condition,
   Such a one or none, fhe faid,
   Who fhould ever her pretty daughter wed.

32. "But no man came, of high condition,
 With a matrimonial propofition,
   And to me it began to be tirefome
   Waiting for fuitors who didn't come.

33. "I therefore thought in fome other manner
 To fave from tarnifh my pride and honour,
   And to meet the handfome young men I flew
   To many a fecret rendez-vous.

34. "Fearing there might be fome mifcarriage,
 Which would perhaps to my future marriage
   Prove an obftacle, if fhe
   Allowed me too much liberty,

35. "My mother took it in contemplation
 To lay on my love-tricks fome limitation,
   And by day and by night henceforward took
   Notes of my every ftep and look.

36. "Now though its indulgence was thus prevented
 The paffion itfelf was rather augmented,
   For a ftrictly forbidden fruit will be
   Sought always the more eagerly.

37. " And the greater the hindrance the more the defire,
    So did it with my inclination tranfpire,
       For I fought every opportunity
       To gratify it fecretly.

38. " By night through my window often glided
    Ghofts with flefh and bones provided,
       Which then would ufually half the night
       Stay with me till morning light.

39. " And when I happened to find nothing better
    I got now and then a love-letter
       Of fuch heart-breaking tenor, as we
       Daily in every romance may fee.

40. " My nineteenth year had exactly ended
    When I one evening a ball attended,
       And there with a gentleman acquainted became
       Herr Baron Von Hogier was his name."

41. Hieronimus here interrupted her talking;
    " Herr Von Hogier ? the thing is fhocking !
       His name, as well as his rank, the whole
       Is familiar enough to me, by my foul !

42. " Herr Von Hogier was a fharper, I tell ye !"
    " He was *all of that*," refumed Amelia,
       " And, dear Hieronimus, you fhall fee
       What took place between him and me.

43. " To Herr Von Hogier I took a great liking,
    His perfon and manners were very ftriking,
       His elegant drefs and great peruke
       At the very firft moment my fancy took.

44. " He made me a very flattering propofal
    Placed his hand and fortune at my difpofal,
    And what pleafed and flattered me far more,
    I was his only angel, he fwore.

45. " He alfo faid much of his goods and poffeffions
    Situated in the land of the Heffians,
    Though he now was travelling to and fro
    Through the world incognito.

46. " He did alfo diftinctly inftruct me
    He'd like, if I pleafed, from home to abduct me,
    If I at the hour appointed would ftand
    Ready, with money and jewels in hand.

47. " And fo, by night, when nothing hindered,
    The coffers and chefts at home I plundered,
    Pocketed what I found without fear
    And took my flight with Herr Von Hogier.

48. " We made our retreat in very good order,
    'Till we about reached the laft Swabian border;
    And during the firft four days of our ride,
    Did not reft twelve hours, I'm fatisfied.

49. " What my parents thought, and how aftounded,
    To find bags empty and daughter abfconded,
    And how they took on and fwore and ftormed,
    You may well imagine but cannot be informed.

50. " When we at laft arrived at W,
    (Not with too long a ftory to trouble you)
    We determined to tarry fome days there
    To reft ourfelves and get good fare.

51. " We, therefore, as we propofed to, tarried,
    And lived as cofy as if we were married,
        And the Herr Baron Von Hogier
        Behaved very tenderly to his dear.

52. " I therefore was now, in my own opinion,
    Happier than a Queen in her dominion,
        And thought of nothing but joy and glee
        And pleafure and feftivity.

53. " But clofe on my heels was misfortune purfuing,
    For before I could dream of anything brewing,
        Suddenly and fecretly one night
        Herr Von Hogier, *per poft*, took flight.

54. " My money, too, dear Hieronimus, (think on't,)
    And my jewels were gone to the dogs in an inftant,
        And of the valuables the whole
        Which I from my parents before had ftole.

55. " I faw now, with all his cooing and billin',
    That Herr Von Hogier was a fettled villain,
        And that matters did not rightly ftand
        With his eftate in the Heffian land.

56. " You can therefore eafily imagine
    How much I took this thing in dudgeon,
        For I had not dreamed that the Herr Von Hogier
        Could be guilty of fuch tricks as this 'ere.

57. " Now left alone and by all forfaken,
    I knew not what ftep was next to be taken,
        And in defperation I looked around
        To fee where a refuge could be found

58. " That I fhould go back again to **my parents**
Was an impoffible occurrence,
 For fuch a courfe would certainly
 Have been very uncomfortable to me.

59. " However I ftill, as a flight confolation,
Had twenty-four ducats remaining in my poffeffion,
 Which I, in cafe of future diftrefs,
 Had fewed into **my under-drefs.**

60. " Thefe twenty-four ducats, I now bethought me,
A fpecial fortune feems to have brought me,
 For **they are now,** moft certainly,
 All **my eftate and property.**

61. " I would not any longer tarry
But after Herr Von Hogier hurry,
 And on the very felf-fame day,
 I took the ftage and drove away.

62. " For I had at the poft-houfe received information
That he hired an extra for the occafion,
 And was therefore probably by this,
 In Swabia, as one might guefs.

63. " If at that time I could have caught him,
To juftice I at once would have brought him,
 And I fhould certainly have then
 Got all my money back again.

64. " It **was, my** dear, in this occupation,   ·
That on the well remembered occafion,
 I found in the ftage coach a fad young man,
 With whom my acquaintance then firft began.

65. " For the reſt, up to this time I have never
    Succeeded in getting any glimpſe whatever,
        Nor have ſo much as been able to hear
        Of the whereabouts of Herr Von Hogier."

66. Here Hieronimus could not help breaking
    In once again on Amelia ſpeaking :
        " Potz tauſend ! I know well," he ſaid,
        Where Herr Von Hogier the ſcamp has fled.

67. " Shortly before our acquaintance, dear Amelia !
    Herr Von Hogier, the son of Belial,
        Spunged me out of much money one day
        At a tavern by his tricky play.

68. " This was the principal occaſion
    Of my melancholy ſituation
        Of mind, which I at laſt forgot
        When in the ſtage by your ſide I ſot.

69. " Herr Von Hogier, too, was one of the couple
    Of travellers, diſguiſed as merchant people,
        Who after ſupper at the inn
        Stole my money bag and all therein.

70. " The robber too, whom I killed, (as already
    Stated,) when I ſaved the gentleman and lady,
        Was verily, by his perſon and face,
        No other than this ſame ſcape-grace.

71. " You, therefore, now may reſt contented :
    His future villanies are prevented,
        And I have thus moſt righteouſly
        Avenged myſelf for his knavery."

72. Amelia replied : " Thy histories,
   My dear ! are full of curious myſteries,
      And ſo remarkable each **event**,
      It fills me with aſtoniſhment !

73. " The proverb : *what is ſpun however finely,*
   Is ſure to come to the ſunlight finally,
      Turns out exactly to a hair
      In the case of that raſcal Hogier there.

74. " But to proceed in my own narration,
   At the time of our ſudden ſeparation,
      On account of the watch I concluded to go on,
      A while, on foot, and all alone.

75. " About that time, by good luck's providing,
   An elderly gentleman came riding
      Along in his carriage, and when he ſpied
      Me trudging on by the roadſide,

76. " With ſuch a ſignificant ſmile he beckoned,
   That I was ſitting by him in a ſecond ;
      And, as my perſon pleaſed him, he
      Made a propoſition to me :

77. " To be his chambermaid, and aid him
   Drive off the blues that did often invade him,
      For he lived alone without any wife,
      And was an old bachelor for life.

78. " Now it would have been dangerous, I concluded,
   And certainly I ſhould be deluded,
      (So the thing began now to appear,)
      To ſeek any further for Herr Von Hogier.

14

79. " And fo I could not make refufal
    To the old gentleman's kind propofal,
        Although his age and his gray hair,
        Were not juft fuch as I wifhed they were.

80. " So I took up with him my habitation
    And gave him effectual confolation,
        And I behaved myfelf to him
        As if I his lawful fpoufe had been.

81. " He therefore held me in high eftimation,
    And gave me the whole houfe-adminiftration,
        And all the fervants, maids and men,
        Subjected to my regimen.

82. " I superintended cellars and preffes,
    Kitchen and chamber and wardrobe and dreffes,
        Saw to the wafhing, table and bed,
        And everything that came under that head.

83. " The keys of the chefts, the plates and platters,
    And even the more valuable matters,
        The linen and filver, were to me
        Committed into cuftody.

84. " And from many an evening till the morrow,
    I beguiled the old gentleman of his forrow,
        And gave his troubled fpirit eafe
        And miniftered to his neceffities.

85. " For the old gentleman would never
    Do the leaft thing without me whatever,
        And nothing in any department,
        Could ever take place without my consent.

86. " Of courfe, in addition to my compenfation,
    I received from him many a valuable donation,
      And, to make up any deficiency,
      I ftole a trifle occafidnally.

87. " Although now nothing external was wanting,
    There was fomething always my fpirit haunting,
      And the time feemed long when I began
      To live with the old gentleman.

88. " 'Tis true in the courfe of time the houfe-writer
    Did make my fpirits a little lighter,
      But, being rather fickly, he
      Was not very interefting to me.

89. " I found it for my comfort neceffary,
    After his death to get a new fecretary,
      And you, my dear, juft then applied
      For the vacant place of the one who had died.

90. " I had for you a prepofeffion,
    At the very firft fight, I muft make the confeffion;
      And this, you fee, was the reafon why
      I fpoke in your favour fo earneftly.

91. " Of all the things that between us tranfpired,
    From the time that you were firft hired
      'Till the night he found you in my room,
      Dear Hieronimus! you are aware, I prefume.

92. " When he at that time difmiffed you,
    I need not fay how much I miffed you,
      But the old man continued all the more
      To give fharp hints on that very fcore.

93. " His anger did my fpirits gall fo,
       That I came very near leaving alfo,
           And it was about as much as I could do
           With my careffes to bring him to.

94. " Meanwhile, from that time, his inclination
       For me gave place to alienation,
           And to a new young kitchen maid
           All his attention henceforth he paid.

95. " And therefore to relieve the depreffion
       Of fpirits your abfence did occafion,
           I lived thenceforward fomewhat free
           With the old gentleman's lackéy.

96. " But when our intercourfe he did difcover,
       All chance of reconciliation was over,
           No word of excufe would he wait to hear—
           I muft pack up my duds at once and clear.

97. " Being now with money tolerably provided,
       To travel through the world I decided,
           'Till fome new opportunity
           Of future fupport fhould turn up for me.

98. " While through this neighborhood I wandered
       A band of players I encountered,
           And at my requeft the company
           For a new actrefs accepted me.

99. " Already fome months have I been ftaying
       With them and in their fervice playing
           Exceedingly well, as I'm inclined
           To think, the parts to me affigned.

100. " For the reſt, it gratifies me greatly
      To think of the good luck that lately
         Has brought together you and me
         For the third time ſo happily."

CHAPTER XXXIII.

How Hieronimus conceived a defire to be a play-actor,
and how he was perfuaded thereto by Mifs Amelia.

HIERONIMUS exceedingly wondered
    At the ftory told in the previous hundred
        Verfes, and quite forgot, from this day,
        His patron and Bavaria.

2. He now determined that he never
    Would leave Amelia on any account whatever,
        And confequently took it in view
        That he would be a comedian too.

3. When Amelia got information
    Of this, fhe approved his determination,
        And extolled her profeffion's dignity
        In the following apology :

4. "I know from many an example,
    That the ftage-player's profeffion has ample
        Claim to be called the worthieft
        Of all that in the world exift.

5. "For the theatre holds up a mirror
    In which one fees, even plainer and clearer
        Than in the world itfelf, how odd
        Is the mixture in life of good and bad.

6. " Now we have merry comedies,
   And now we have tearful tragedies;
      Now they laugh and dance and fing,
      And now figh and groan and all that fort of thing.

7. " Now comical farces excite our laughter,
   Now tears and bloodfhed follow right after;
      Now one is poor and now he's rich:
      To-day in the parlor, the next in the ditch.

8. " Now he's a peafant and now he's a ruler,
   Now he's a fool and now he's a fcholar;
      Now he is young and now he is old,
      Now he is warm and now he is cold.

9. " Now he is fober, now he is tipfy,
   Now he's a capuchin, now he's a gipfy;
      Now he's a beggar and now he's a bar·n,
      Now he's a varlet and now a Herr Von.

10. " Now a renownift and now a lackey,
    Now a chamberlain and now a blackey;
       Now a landlord and now a gueft,
       Now a cowherd and now a prieft.

11. " Now a paftor—a philofopher famous,
    Now a fexton—an ignoramus;
       Now a monarch and now a fudge,
       Now a hangman and now a judge.

12. " Through thefe and other fimilar changes,
    One, ever newly delighted, ranges,
       And the courfe of the world is faithfully
       Reprefented in all its variety.

13. " If we only play with all our powers
      The parts which for the time are ours,
        The audience applaud at the end
        With a vehement clapping of the hand.

14. " On the contrary, when we fail or blunder,
      The audience is down on us like thunder
        The pit and galleries all laugh,
        And hiſs and yell and hoot us off."

15. " Your account, dear Amelia, I cannot deny it,
      Pleaſes me ſo, I'm diſpoſed to try it,"
        Anſwered with a hearty buſs
        The new play-actor Hieronimus.

16. He was now to the manager preſented
      And to him by Amelia recommended,
        And on the next day following he
        Was enrolled in the acting company.

CHAPTER XXXIV.

How Hieronimus became a real player, and how **Mifs**
Amelia was falfe to **him** *and ran off with a rich*
gentleman, and how he alfo in defperation went away.

INDULGENT reader! thou fhalt now be inftrućted
How in his new profeffion Hieronimus condućted,
    When once the manager had tried
    His qualifications, and was fatisfied.

2. Drunken ftudents and profligate preachers,
Laughable fextons and ftupid teachers,
    Secretaries amoroufly inclined,
    Poltroons and rakes, and parts of that kind.

3. All thefe Hieronimus played to perfećtion,
Becaufe for fuch he'd a natural predilećtion,
    And every time he appeared therein,
    A general round of applaufe did win.

4. And when an author he did enaćt, or
Appeared in a fchoolmafter's charaćter,
    Now and then one feemed to fee
    The author or fchoolmafter bodily.

5. But when the philofopher's part he affected,
   No great applaufe could be expected,
     And in fentimental paftoral
     Hieroniimus was juft next to nothing at all.

6. He played the fine gentleman very badly,
   And, as a general thing, failed fadly
     In any thing like a refpectable part,
     Or where there was much to be got by heart.

7. Hieronimus in this new employment
   Experienced unalloyed enjoyment,
     And blifsfully flew the moments away
     In the arms of his queen—his Amelia.

8. He would not in his love-intoxication
   Have exchanged for a king's his fituation,
     And all his trouble and forrow, at laft,
     Seemed to be over and ended and paft.

9. But how very feldom one of us liftens
   To the proverb " All is not gold that gliftens."
     Fortune often takes a freak
     And plays us an unexpected trick.

10. Hieronimus (as you'll fee by what fhall follow)
    Was fated to find her promifes hollow,
      For when he leaft dreamed of fuch a thing,
      The greateft joy of his life took wing

11. The forrow by which he was now o'ertaken
    The heavieft of all he did reckon,
      Namely, his moft dearly beloved
      Amelia unfaithful proved.

12. It happened thus: on a certain occafion
    A rich young gentleman of confideration,
      Saw the enchanting Amelia
      Perform at the theatre in a play.

13. Now as there are ninnies all the world over,
    He immediately became her lover,
      And Amelia was fhrewd enough
      Not to treat him with a rebuff.

14. In reading her hiftory we eafily discover
    That fhe had a great inclination, moreover,
      (Becaufe fhe was a woman, you fee)
      To frequent change and variety.

15. The rich young man frequent vifits paid her,
    For which Hieronimus did upbraid her,
      His face grew black and his eyes grew red,
      And in his defpair he wifhed himfelf dead.

16. But that only made him lefs amiable
    To Amelia, and daily more intolerable,
      And very foon he received from her
      A renunciation *formaliter*.

17. When this blight fell on his affeftions,
    He at once diffolved his theatrical connexions,
      And in extreme defperation of mind
      Left the fcene of difgrace behind.

18. That we here may bring the narration
    Of Amelia's life to a termination,
      She left with the gentleman, and it is faid,
      Died two years after in child-bed.

CHAPTER XXXV.

How Hieronimus returned home to Schildburg, and how
he found there all forts of changes.

AND fo Hieronimus was fated
   To wander again, as above narrated,
     And never before in his life had he
     Set out fo difcontentedly.

2. Amelia's unlooked for infidelity
   Seemed every hour a new reality,
     And in his defpair he could fcarcely keep
     Himfelf from taking the fatal leap.

3. 'Tis true, if I may exprefs an opinion,
   His patron in the Bavarian dominion
     Would have been, in his prefent afflicted ftate,
     His fureft refuge from adverfe fate.

4. But one who falls into tribulation
   Is apt to lofe his felf-poffeffion,
     And at fuch times, ('tis the general rule,)
     Refigns his wits and acts the fool.

5. And fo in utter defperation
   Hieronimus formed the determination
     That he would now his fteps retrace
     To Schildeburg, his native place.

6. And now as he met with no detention
   On his journey homeward, worthy of mention,
   He did at laſt, thank Heaven! arrive
   At the place of his deſtination, alive.

7. Here, when the firſt ſalutations were over,
   He very ſoon began to diſcover
   That many changes had taken place
   In his long abſence from the place.

8. His mother, indeed, he found ſtill living,
   But in outward circumſtances far from thriving,
   Indeed her means were very ſtrait,
   And her bread was earned with trouble great.

9. He learned with ſorrow, that one brother
   Had gone the way of all fleſh, another
   Had opened a little Nuremberg ſhop,
   Whereby he managed to fill his crop.

10. The eldeſt brother had ſuccefsfully courted
    The uglieſt woman the country ſupported,
    But the money which ſhe did poſſefs
    Made him forget her uglinefs.

11. He alſo learned that his eldeſt ſiſter
    Had connected herſelf in marriage with Miſter
    Kircher, the ſexton of the place,
    And lived with him in pretty good caſe.

12. His ſiſter Gertrude one Mr. Geier
    Had wedded, and become a father by her,
    But thereupon was off like the wind,
    And left both bride and infant behind.

15

13. She tried her beſt to earn her living,
     Her ſervices indiſcriminately giving
        To young people of the richer ſort,
        From whom ſhe thus received a ſupport.

14. Another ſiſter, they did inform him,
     An old widower took to keep houſe and warm him,
        And, in ſo far, appeared to be
        Living with him in peace and unity.

15. And, laſt of all, his younger ſiſter,
     A blooming maiden, whoſe name was Eſther,
        Did ſtill to her mother ſolace afford,
        And get from her her daily board.

16. Now, Hieronimus's return made his mother
     Very happy, and no doubt, each ſiſter and brother,
        Becauſe they ſo long had not ſeen him, nor heard
        Of his whereabouts a ſingle word:

17. Still, at the ſame time, it would not do for
     Him to be living at home as a loafer,
        And ſo they began to take in view
        What buſineſs there was Hieronimus might do.

CHAPTER XXXVI.

*How Hieronimus became a night-watchman in Schild-
burg, and how his mother's dream and Mrs. Urgalindina's prophecy were fulfilled.*

NOW it came to pafs that the **man they hired**
   As watchman in Schildburg had lately **expired,**
     And fo the office was lying void,
     Vacant, empty and unfupplied.

2. As, now, in all ſtates that are ordered rightly,
   The watchman can't be diſpenſed with nightly ;
   　The burghers conſulted in the preſent cafe
   　On ordaining another to fill his place.

3. Now many fit ſubjects might have been ſelected
   Who to taking the office would not have objected,
   　But, on account of his powerful voice,
   　Hieronimus ſeemed to be their choice.

4. 'Tis true ſome perſons at firſt made objections
   And caſt upon him perſonal reflections,
   　As if Hieronimus would not do
   　Exactly for the office in view.

5. For the city would not, ſo they contended,
   If he were watchman, be well defended,
   　For how could he who preferred to ſleep
   　When he ought to wake, the city keep ?

6. Neverthelefs did Hieronimus
   Very ſoon receive a unanimous
   　Invitation from the *bourgeoiſie*
   　That he would the new night-watchman be.

7. But firſt it would be neceſſary
   His predeceſſor's widow he ſhould marry,
   　For the deceaſed had ſtood very high
   　In the city's eſteem deſervedly.

8. And ſo, by way of compenſation
   To his highly afflicted widow, the corporation
   　To the other qualifications tacked on
   　The marrying of her perſon as a *ſine qua non.*

9. Now, as her age was thirty only,
And her perfon certainly not very homely,
   Hieronimus accepted the terms propofed
   And his predeceffor's widow efpoufed.

10. And now to old and young, as they flumbered,
The hours of night were again muſically numbered,
   For Hieronimus, the new
   Watchman put his horn to his mouth and blew.

11. And whenever the clock was heard from the tower,
He began as follows to call the hour:
   " Hark ye, gentlemen, as ye lie there ſtill,
   And hear what I to you ſing and tell :

12. " The clock has juſt proclaimed the hour,
Twelve, one, two, three, from the old church tower;
   Take care, if I may you advife,
   Of fire and light and your daughters likewife !

13. " That no one may fet anything on fire,
Or any other harm may tranfpire,
   Be careful, therefore, and fee to 't,
   To 't, to 't, to 't, toot! toot! toot ! toot ! "

14. For the reſt he ſteadily conducted
Himfelf as a watchman well inſtructed ;
   Slept foundly all day long that he
   Might at night more wakeful be.

15. In all the time of his ſinging and watching
No thief dared riſk his power of catching,
   So that Schildburg was entirely free
   From all nocturnal burglary.

16. And every citizen, however foundly fnoring,
    Woke when Hieronimus his blaft was pouring,
      And the found of his horn and his nightly call
      Were heard throughout the town by all.

17. A wonderful coincidence this muft be reckoned
    With Frau Jobs's dream (in chapter fecond,)
      And all turns out, to a hair, for us
      In the cafe of the watch Hieronimus.

18. And that which Urgalindina ftated,
    When about the boy's future interrogated,
      On the ground of chiromantic art,
      Was verified now in every part.

19. Now that the things were fulfilled completely,
    The explanation could be made very neatly,
      As with prophecies is always the cafe;
      They're myfteries till the event takes place.

20. Meantime Frau Schnepperle's talk (remember)
    When Frau Jobs was keeping child-chamber,
      (As may be read in chapter 3)
      Has not as yet been fulfilled, you fee.

21. And, from our prefent information,
    We fhould fay that Frau Schnepperle's reputation
      In the matter of phyfiognomy
      Muft fuffer very confiderably.

CHAPTER XXXVII.

*How Hieronimus received a visit from friend Death,
who took him to his rest. A chapter which would do
for a funeral sermon.*

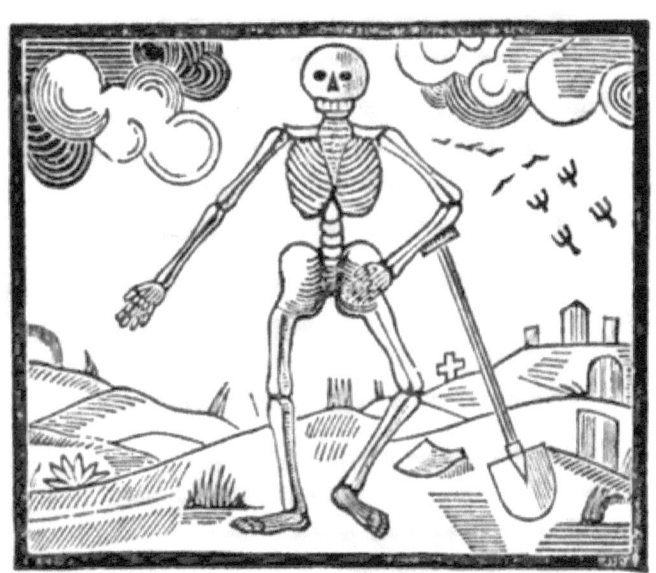

T HERE'S a fenfible faying which, for ages,
   As is very well known to all of us fages,
      Through learned books has run its round,
      (In the old church-father Horace 'tis found :)

2. *As well againſt the palace portals,*
   As againſt the doors of the pooreſt mortals,
     Friend Death, who is everywhere well-known,
     Knocks with his old dry knuckle-bone.

3. That is, when popularly tranſlated,
   All that lives to die is fated,
     As well the monarch as the boor,
     As well the rich man as the poor.

4. Inasmuch as friend Death makes not the ſmalleſt
   Diſtinction between the loweſt and talleſt,
     But cuts down all both low and high,
     With the ſtricteſt impartiality.

5. And, as he ever ſlyly watches,
   The cavalier and the clown he catches,
     The beggar and alſo the great Sultán,
     The tailor and alſo the Tartar Khan.

6. And with his ſcythe his rounds he goeth
   And honorables and lackeys moweth,
     The herdsmaid and the titled dame,
     Without diſtinction of place or name.

7. He liſtens to no compromiſes;
   Both crowns and bag-wigs he deſpiſes,
     Doctor's hats and ſtag's horns
     And whatever elſe men's heads adorns.

8. A thouſand things he has command of,
   By which he us can make an end of,
     And now the dagger, and now the peſt,
     And now a grape-ſtone, gives us reſt.

9. A ſickneſs now and now a panic,
   And now a miſtaken doſe of arſénic,
      Poiſon or pleaſure or very ſpite,
      Or love or grief or a mad dog's bite.

10. Now a law-ſuit and now a ſplinter,
    Now a bad woman and now a bad winter,
       Now a nooſe or other ſnare,
       Of which may Heaven help us beware.

11. Againſt his darts, when they aſſail us,
    No d'Arçon's floating batteries 'll avail us,
       Friend Death, the ravenous, is not ſcared
       By cannon or fortreſs, ſhield or ſword.

12. The commandant of the Seven Towers,
    The grand vizier in his harem's bowers,
       As well as Diogenes in his tub,
       All—all are ſwallowed by him for grub.

13. So is it as far as memory reaches,
    As far as ancient hiſtory teaches;
       Jacob Böhme and Ariſtotlés,
       Klaus Narre and Demoſthenes;

14. Misſhapen Eſop his fables tellin',
    And the Grecian beauty, world-famed Helen,
       Unhappy Job and King Solomon,
       Gave up the ghoſt and now are gone.

15. Emperor Max and Jobs the Senátor
    Virgil and Hans Sachs my ancéſtor,
       Goliath great and David ſmall,
       Early or late, they periſhed all.

16. Nicholas Klimm and Marcus Aurelius,
    Cato and Eulenſpiegelius,
      Ritter Samſon and old Don
      Quixote, alas, they are dead and gone.

17. **Kartouche** and King Alexander together,
    As like each other as birds of a feather,
      Bramarbas the hero and Hannibal,
      Met the common deſtiny all.

18. Great Auguſtus, alſo Poland's
    Hero and Charles XII., nolens volens,
      As well as the Perſian Shah Kulikan
      And Czar Peter, that famous man ;

19. **Item,** Xerxes, with his hoſt ſo enormous,
    Potiphar, of whom the ſcriptures inform us,
      And Polyphemus, the one-eyed,
      And old Methuſalem have died.

20. **All—all—to the** grave they had to carry,
    Calvin and Father Santa Clara,
      Likewiſe the Patriach Abraham
      And alſo Eraſmus of Rotterdam.

21. **Müller** Arnold, too, and the Ruſſian
    Imperial Dynaſty and the Pruſſian
      Lawyers, and April, well known,
      Who fell down ſtairs at Ratiſbon.

22. All—all—have ſunk beneath his ſickle,
    Hippocrates Magnus and Schuppachs Michel,
      Galenus and Doctor Menadie,
      With the Salernian Academy ;

23. Not one of them found time for fleein',
Not Noftradamus nor fuperintendent Ziehen :
 With doctor Fauft, dreamer Swedenburg, too,
 He made a clean fweep and went through.

24. Orpheus, the great mufician,
Molière, the comedian of the Parifian nation,
 And the famous painter Apellés,
 Friend Death has fwept away all thefe.

25. The long-eared Midas, (all children know it,)
Homerus, the old blind beggar-poet,
 Veftris the dancer and brave Tamerlane,
 Struggled with the deftroyer in vain.

26. **Ah** yes, dear reader! with terrible grip he
Seized and devoured Penelope, Xanthippe,
 Judith, Dido, Lucretia,
 And the queen from far Arabia.

27. Cynic Timon, Democritus the laughing phyfician,
Juggler Schröpfer and Simon the magician,
 Socrates and young Werther, the one
 A wife man, t'other a fimpleton.

28. Bucephalus and Roffinante
And Abulabas the Elephant, he,
 With the horfe Bayard and Balaam's **afs,**
 Took for a morning meal like grafs.

29. Summa Summarum, the long and the fhort is,
That in none of the chronicles do we find notice,
 That friend Death has ever any one paffed
 Without coming back for him at laft.

30. And what he has not eaten already
  He will not fail to remember when he's ready :
    Alas! dear reader, alfo thee,
    And, what is worft of all, even me !

31. From the common lot (we've now to mention,)
  Hieronimus, the watchman, found no exemption,
    Him, too, friend Death removed from the ftage,
    When forty years and three weeks of age.

32. He caught an inflammatory fever
  From which he might have recovered, however,
    If they had only let natûre
    That beft of nurfes, work his cure.

33. But a doctor who in curing was mighty,
  With a powerful dofe of Elixir Vitæ,
    In the very beft method carried him faft
    To the place where we all muft go at laft.

34. And now when to the grave they bore him,
  The Schildeburgers did loudly deplore him,
    For there had not, in many a century,
    Been known fuch a famous night watchman as he.

NOTE.

One is reminded by this chapter of " Father Mulvaney's Sarmon" in Mrs. Hall's Lights and Shadows of Irifh Life : " Now you fee that the great min of *ould* times are all dead ! not a mortial fowl of them all alive." . . . . .

" There was Julus Cafar and twelve of them there was— *mortus est*—he's dead !" . . . . .

" There was the great Cleopatra, an Egyptian, and a great warrior ; he ufed to drink *purls* for *wather—mortus est !* he's dead too ! There was Marc Anthony, a grate frind and coajuthor of Cleopatra's, he had a grate turn for boating and the like—*mortus est*—he's dead too ! There was Charley-mange, a grate Frinch man of larning and tongues, and with all his larning—*mortus est*—he's dead too ! There was the grate Alexandre the gineral of the whole wide world—*mortus est*—he's dead too ! . . . There was the grate Cicero, a mighty fine pracher like myself—*mortus est*—he's dead too !"

FIN—